Joanna Whitmire was born and raised in the Deep South. A college graduate with a minor in English and degrees in both biology and fine arts, she worked as an educator for many years. She loves art, music, books, movies, soap operas, her family and friends, our beautiful Earth, and animals, especially her own. She still lives in her hometown.

This book is dedicated to dreamers and gentle souls, to those kind hearts who want to save the world, and to those lost souls who are searching to find their way, or themselves. Persevere and be brave.

Joanna Whitmire

I FOUND ME

AUSTIN MACAULEY PUBLISHERS™

LONDON • CAMBRIDGE • NEW YORK • SHARJAH

Ordering Information
Quantity sales: Special discounts are available on quantity purchases by corporations, associations, and others. For details, contact the publisher at the address below.

Publisher's Cataloging-in-Publication data
Whitmire, Joanna
I Found Me

ISBN 9781645758358 (Paperback)
ISBN 9781645758365 (Hardback)
ISBN 9781645758372 (ePub e-book)

Library of Congress Control Number: 2021907614

www.austinmacauley.com/us

First Published (2021)
Austin Macauley Publishers LLC
40 Wall Street, 33rd Floor, Suite 3302
New York, NY 10005
USA

mail-usa@austinmacauley.com
+1 (646) 5125767

I would like to thank my family and friends for their encouragement and support. In particular: my sisters, who are also my comrades and friends; the Ladies of the Grape, who are my anchors, and the girls at the hair salon, who helped me *Steel Magnolias* style. Also, thank you to some friends who made me feel special and empowered: Barbara, DDR, Mary, Diana, Judith, Paul, Peter, Ned, and Bert. Also, thank you to everyone at Austin Macauley for their help, support, and faith in me.

Chapter One

This will probably be as true and as honest a narrative as you will ever read or hear, because I lived it. I want to begin by admitting that I have made some very foolish mistakes in my life, and they all involved silly ideas, poor judgment, and dating the wrong boys. I always had a weakness for "bad boys", but then, who doesn't. But I was never, ever foolish enough to think that I was beautiful. However, I did think that I was cute. And boys always like cute girls. In fact, I thought that Jack Mallard thought that I was the cutest thing that he had ever laid eyes on. So, the day that I found out, without a doubt, that that was not necessarily so, was the day that changed my life forever.

That day, I stood in stunned disbelief, frozen, as my friend laid out the whole sordid mess for me without leaving out a single hurtful, sickening detail. Betrayal. Abuse. Degradation. Disrespect. Adultery. Belittlement. Humiliation. Almost all of the elements of a Greek tragedy – all, that is, except murder. But maybe shredding someone's heart counts for that. But as awful as these truths were, the most devastating, the most mind-numbing, the most paralyzing was the realization that Jack Mallard didn't really think that I was the cutest thing that he had ever laid eyes on.

*****

When Jack and I met, it was a dark and stormy night. Just kidding, actually, it was an unbelievably beautiful, balmy, late-spring evening at a friend's beach house party. When my eyes met Jack Mallard's turquoise-blue eyes, I was a goner. He was everything I had ever dreamed of: handsome, athletic, confident, smart, educated, and from a supposedly nice family. He had great hair and was a fantastic dancer. And he had a great laugh! So, what was not to love? I thought that we were made for each other. But then, I was also a naive, hopeless romantic.

Happily, my parents seemed to really take to Jack, although they had some reservations about some of his family, but did not discuss it with me. I guess they didn't want to ruin my starry-eyed happiness or burst my bubble. I was thrilled, because I was completely and thoroughly gaga over him, and prayed that he really liked me too! I mean, after all, what was not to like? I was sassy, full of myself, nice, smart, kind, tenderhearted, and of course, cute – with dimples!

Well, as they say, love is blind, and lust is oblivious, and the two together, unfortunately, seem to create a complete lack of commonsense, and a terrible tendency to blindly ignore and overlook flaws or signs of trouble – like his moments of disquieting moods and attitudes that began to surface every so often. Not surprisingly, and needless to say, the worlds we hailed from were quite different, although we both were from families that were well-educated and highly respected (or so I thought). Jack's family, a clan of lawyers and politicians, was relatively new to the county. In fact, quite a few of the town wags quipped "nouveau," and because of the Mallards' grasping and overbearing behavior, quite a few of the county "grande dames" would sniff "carpetbaggers and opportunists!"

On the other hand, my family was one of the oldest families in the county, dating back to before the Revolutionary War. We were well-thought of, even when we suffered huge financial reversals. My world was quite splendid: books, dogs, horses, horses, horses, horse shows, and pony club. Our days were filled with family afternoons of badminton, croquet, playing with cats and dogs, and you guessed it, riding horses. We were kind, gentle, thoughtful people, taught to be gracious, fair, and respectful to one and all. So, it is no surprise that I did not know what to expect when I stepped from my sunny world into the murky world of politics, cocktail parties, fundraisers, backslapping, ass-kissing, harassment, and intimidation – a lamb to the slaughter.

*****

Now, perhaps it is time that you get a description of where we lived our lives, because, as you know, where someone lives is tantamount as to how that person lives. As you have probably already surmised, we lived in a small, seemingly sleepy, southern town; underneath its facade of quiet civility, it was a buzzing, humming hive of activity and gossip, tended by do-gooders and busybodies (many of whom are relatives of mine), as well as many lovely people (again, many are my relatives; remember, my family has been here forever). The town is the county seat of a very rural county, made up of farms and countless plantations, where the main source of income is connected, in some way, to some aspect of the timber business, and the largest employer is the public school system. The lifestyles and hobbies of most of the residents involve hunting, fishing, overeating, and dabbling in other peoples' business. But this is my "briar patch," where I was born and raised. We, my family and I, lived out in the country on a horse farm in a rambling old farmhouse that was built in the late 1800s by my great-grandfather, after the original old home place had burned.

Most of the county lies about forty miles inland from the Atlantic Ocean, so the countryside is slightly rolling with either dense forests and vegetation, large fields for farming, or dark, brooding cypress swamps. It is lush with every type of tree, shrub, or flower found in a hot, humid climate. It represents an incomparably beautiful combination of Deep South meets the Tropics. Stately, moss-laden oaks and towering pines live happily with fragrant magnolias and sturdy palmettos, along with an abundance of ferns. Every species and variety, type and color, of flowering plant blooms in a wild abandon of mixtures of riotous colors. Entangled vines of jasmine, morning glories, honeysuckles, and wisteria cover and drape over other plants, fences, and buildings. Ivy spreads along on walls, along the ground and walkways, and up into the trees. All of this lends a gloriously jubilant air of hidden secrets and decadence.

Lush and beautiful, it is hot and humid in the summer, and bone-chillingly damp in the winter. Black-water rivers flow through the area, carrying water to the ocean. Creeks and ponds dot the countryside, many of them emptying into the rivers or into dark, mysterious cypress and hardwood swamps. The area teems with wildlife of every type and variety, too numerous to recite – a roll call and testament to a Noah's Ark of God's creatures. The county is also home to hordes, nests, infestations, and swarms of every type of insect, especially those that bite and sting.

The town itself is nestled in the center of all of this splendor. Jack grew up in town in a beautiful antebellum house, with wrap-around porches. His parents bought the house when they moved to the area. In fact, this is where Jack and I lived for most of our married life. It was, and still is, a grand place – quite spectacular, sitting smack-dab in the middle of town, surrounded by a huge, shady yard.

*****

Now that you have a mental image of the setting of this melodrama, it is time to introduce you to some of the cast of characters. I have already briefly described Jack, who was not only gorgeous, but was also, at one time, fun, fun, fun. He was never all bad, in fact, he actually had a kind side to him. He just let inner demons control him, at times, and let them release his dark side. Nevertheless, to me, he was the best of his family. By the time I had married, my siblings had moved away to find, and live, their own lives; and my sweet parents had passed away. Jack and I waited to get married because I was taking care of my parents and my baby brother. I helped them, and ran the farm, while also teaching school. My dreams of becoming an illustrator were exchanged for dreams for my brother. Our father succumbed to lung cancer, and my mother, an invalid, passed away several years later. I then waited a little longer until my brother could fulfill his aspirations to enter medical school – Mama and Daddy would have been so proud! So, I was pretty much alone in this world, except for the new family that marriage provided me. I worked very hard to become a viable part of the family. After all, this was to be the new chapter of my life. A new beginning!

Now, do not think that I think I am so perfect that I can cast stones, not so. Because, of course, I was, and am, as flawed as anyone – but I'm not mean. I would never try to paint myself as an icon of perfection. Although laidback and easy-going, I can be obstinate, stubborn, and a little impatient, at times. But in my family, I had always been an avid daydreamer, and the merry one who joked and cavorted about to make everyone else laugh. Mama always said that I had a sunny, cheerful disposition, but Daddy also warned that I was way too sensitive to criticism and too easily crushed, probably because I was, and am, an inveterate dreamer, and always believe in, and hope for, the happy ending. But I could sometimes be a pouter. There's actually quite an art to it. However, my pouting spells were always brief – they were over as soon as someone or something made me laugh, which was usually pretty easy to do. Being mad and holding grudges are just too exhausting and pointless. One last trait that I mightily embraced, and that identified me, is that I considered it my mission in life to take in, rescue, raise, save, or nurse any of God's creatures that needed help or a home, resulting in quite a menagerie of "all creatures great and small." My older sister, sarcastically, but with grudging admiration, dubbed me "Jesus Christ of the Animal World" – a nickname that has stayed with me my whole life. One day, when I was kneeling in the bushes giving antibiotics to some kittens that had found their way to me, I didn't hear Jack walk up behind me until I heard him exhale his cigarette smoke. He said, 'You know, you can't save the world.'

I squinted up through the sunlight at him, and said, 'I know that, but I can try to save this little piece.' I gave it my best. But in looking back, maybe I stayed with Jack as long as I did – which was for far too long – through some terrible times, because I sensed that inside of him was a lonely, wounded creature, a lost soul that, for once, try as I may, I could not help.

*****

And so, onward. My marriage introduced a new cast of characters, and jumpstarted my new life. My new life! I embraced my new life and my new beginning. I thought that my marriage would be a "happily-ever-after," and that the rather frightening, disturbing episodes that were already surfacing in our relationship would magically go away, because I was going to be the best wife, the best daughter-in-law, the best sister-in-law, the best aunt, the best everything, ever! Can you tell that I was a naive dreamer and a "cock-eyed optimist"? And someone who had read entirely too many romantic novels and watched way too many romantic movies? Needless to say, I started this new adventure with wide-eyed hopes and delusional expectations. But at least I honestly tried and gave it my best!

I quite liked and respected my mother-in-law and father-in-law, who passed away early in our marriage. Also, I liked my sisters-in-law Myrna Rae and Trudy, and enjoyed their company. However, once I separated from Jack, they dropped me like a hot potato, a scorching hot potato. The nieces and nephews remained relatively neutral (at least to my face) and distant, except for one nephew who felt compelled to shove me up against a wall. A class act!

However, my brothers-in-law (Jack's brothers) are a different story. When the Mallard family genes were handed out, Jack must have received the whole shebang for good looks, as his brothers each bore a distinct resemblance to a troll, or perhaps one of Snow White's dwarfs. I have always felt that their cruel, overbearing boyish pranks and mean-spirited treatment towards their baby brother were the root of Jack's anger issues, alcoholism, and harsh treatment of others. All three of those men, professional and involved with politics, must have specialized in bullying, intimidation, and strong-arm tactics. None of them, Jack included, respected women; they denigrated, belittled, and exploited women whenever and wherever they pleased. In other words, they were pigs in their attitudes towards women (with abject apologies to all swine).

These men, Mark, Bob and Ed, were alcoholics and entitled womanizers. They had a predilection for pornography and treated most women with disrespect disguised in a facade of being Southern gentlemen. Their tactics were very Machiavellian: courtly and charming on the outside, but behind the scenes, reverting to inappropriate touching; suggestive, lewd remarks; and bold attempts to force a kiss. Disgusting and humiliating. My years with the Mallards were spent in an almost orchestrated dance of eluding caresses, ignoring salacious, insulting remarks and fending off attempted kisses.

I would often ask myself, "Why don't you take up for yourself?" I knew that if I told Jack, he would accuse me of enticing or leading these men on. So, why? Shame. Embarrassment. Intimidation. Survival. After a while, guilty silence became a way of life. I no longer recognized myself. Shame on me for not taking up for, if not myself, at least the other girls and women who were being humiliated and exploited. I wondered what had happened to me, the essence of me. Shame on those men. Maybe they thought that wealth and position made them beyond reprimand and common decency, but Mama would have called them "trifling."

Chapter Two

Sadly for me, I have always been someone who loved with her whole heart, never any half-heartedness. This sets one up for a lot of hurt and heartache. I have always loved everything more, be it cats, dogs, or humans. So, as you can imagine, I was absolutely besotted with Jack. Early on, I thought that everything about him was beautiful; he had beautiful russet hair that curled slightly along the ends, and he had beautiful hands. He dressed everyday as if he had stepped out of the Preppy Handbook. He knew anything and everything about music, played several musical instruments, and had a pleasant, mellow voice. He had a wild, courageous, cavalier air about him (bad boy!) that was exhilarating and contagious, and irresistible. And he always smelled good. Maybe he loved me some back, but I know that I loved him more.

During the early days of our relationship, I thought that Jack somewhat resembled Eddy Haskell of the "Leave It to Beaver" days, because he was smarmily pleasant and charming to older adults, but wild and unpredictable with his peers. As time wore on and we began to grow up, he began to resemble Mr. Hyde of Dr. Jekyll and Mr. Hyde, as his wild unpredictability began to take a turn for the dark side.

Fortunately, there is no way possible for me to list or describe all of the miserable, dark, frightening, hurtful moments in our lives together. It would entail and produce a tome the size of the Bible. But I can provide a short synopsis of misery for you. In the early days, Jack's dark side emerged in the form of verbal humiliation, name-calling, and belittlement – usually when he had had too much to drink, which was almost always. Just out of the blue, for no apparent reason, he would criticize my appearance, throw old boyfriends in my face, or one of his favorites, make fun of the fact that my parents had had to sell most of our property to stay afloat and maintain our lifestyle. He loved to say that my family's middle name was "sell." In front of people. Just to embarrass me. I would pretend to shrug it off, and would make a funny joke about it to distract people so that they wouldn't see how hurt I was for myself and for my parents. However, one thing that he never figured out was that the locals didn't care. In our county, my family was "used-tas." In the South, "used-tas" were families that used to have money, old money. Southerners respect "used-tas" and hold them in high regard, much more than new people rolling around in their new money. Jack often called me vulgar names like "pussy-peddling whore" out of the blue, for no sane reason. Sometimes, he would try to set traps for me, to test my fidelity. He must have dated some real winners in the past. I will relate just one of these incidents for you.

It happened when we were dating. One weekend when we were staying at Jack's parents' beach house, Jack had to return to town to attend a wedding to which I had not been invited as I was not a close friend of the couple. Instead of leaving me to hang out and enjoy his beach house, Jack insisted on dropping me off at a house that some of his friends had rented. There was a rowdy crowd there, and Jack asked them to babysit me. I actually had a pleasant time; I sat in the sun, walked on the beach (alone), and ate lunch with the guys. They were very nice. After a while, one of them shamefacedly confessed that Jack had left with instructions for them to "come on to me" so that he could see if I slept with any of them. I thought it was despicable, Jack thought it was funny. What was worse is that I stayed with him! Where was my brain?

When he was annoyed, Jack would often grab me by my wrists or shoulders, squeezing hard and yanking me around. Frighteningly, his tantrums began to escalate. One night when we were still dating, Jack and I were watching television, and all of a sudden, he began to verbally attack me, accusing me of absurd things and belittling me. Sickened, and sick of it all, I jumped up to get dressed and leave. Jack leaped up and grabbed me by my nipples, twisting them as hard as he could. It was excruciating! And it was cruel. I tried to push him away, but he gripped me by my upper arms and began to viciously shake me. When he finally stopped shaking me, he stepped back as he let go of me. I fell backwards and cracked my head on the floor. Concussion #1.

I did not tell anyone at home. I was humiliated and embarrassed, and afraid that my family might not let me see him again. Now, how pathetic and sick is that? Who was I? Where was I? Early the next morning, I went foxhunting with my sister. I had a screaming headache, and was so dizzy that I ended up just hill topping, not even attempting to go over fences. The following day, I felt even worse, so I went to my doctor, who happened to be my cousin, and told him what had happened. Of course, he had to keep it confidential, but he was absolutely outraged. But it gets worse. Since I had to miss a week of work, I lied to my friends and coworkers. I told them that I had received a concussion as the result of a riding accident. The truth was just too awful.

Sometimes, during our early days, I would try to take up for myself, or would still feel sassy enough to talk back. Bad idea. He would quickly quell that; he would grab me and twist my arm behind my back until I thought it would break. Once, when we were at a friend's wedding reception, Jack, as usual, was so drunk that he could barely stand up, much less walk. Miraculously, I somehow managed to get him into the car. It was a small, stick-shift sports car. Jack began to loudly accuse me of embarrassing him by dragging him out of the party. Then he grabbed my right arm – I was in the driver's seat – and twisted my arm behind my back until I cried. My arm was numb and immobile. I thought it might be broken. I had to drive and shift gears with my left arm, while still fending him off. Once again, I was the ultimate enabler, I remained silent. But good news, my arm was not broken.

Another incident took place in the mountains while we were spending the weekend at Jack's cabin. His brother, Ed, and his wife, Myrna Rae, were staying at their mountain house, which was just down the mountain from ours. The four of us attended a sporting event together in a nearby town. Jack and I had left our car at Ed's house so that we could all ride together. We returned late that night; everyone had had a grand time. When we got to Ed's house, Jack and I climbed into Jack's old wagoneer and drove up the mountain to our house. Jack was, big surprise, very drunk, and for some unknown reason, had become very confrontational. He began to insult me, using the most vulgar language imaginable, describing my vagina and what he didn't like about it. I was speechless. When we got to the cabin, he stopped the car and leaped out. I climbed out, and then turned and leaned down into the foot of the car to retrieve a small cooler and my pocketbook. The interior light was not working. I stood back up and turned just as Jack was striding by. He kicked my door, slamming it into my head. I saw a lightning bolt in my head, and then nothing but blackness.

Then, dimly, I could hear Jack's muffled yelling for me to hurry up. It was then that I realized that I was on the ground – and blind. I felt my way up the side of the car to a standing position, and called to Jack, telling him that the car door had hit my head, and that I couldn't see. I was in a panic. I felt him grabbing me and yanking me to the porch. By this time, I had realized that I couldn't see because my eyes were covered with blood. While I stood on the porch, waiting for Jack to open the door, I could hear blood splatting on the floor. Jack finally opened the door and dragged me into the bathroom. He bent me over the tub and poured a pitcher of water over my face. Not one kind or concerned word left his mouth. He was furious over the inconvenience. Thankfully, the blood was coming from a cut over my eye, my eyes were okay. Instead of consoling

22

me or trying to medicate me, or at least acting pleased that I wasn't blind, Jack began to shout, warning me to not tell anyone what had happened. I stood and unsteadily tried to leave the room. Huge mistake. Jack lunged after me and began to wrestle with me, shaking me, twisting my arm, and swearing me to silence.

The next morning, we drove to his brother's house for a planned day of sightseeing. Ed and Myrna Rae immediately spotted the cut over my eye and the bruises on my face and the side of my head. But like a true enabler, I fobbed it off as my clumsiness, that I had slipped and hit my head on the car door. Then as we walked towards the cars, they saw the blood on the side of the car. Once again, I made light of the incident, and we set off on our sightseeing tour. As we rode along the winding roads, my headache became unbearable, and I felt dizzy and lightheaded. Then the double vision started; I waited as long as I could, hoping it would go away. It didn't. Finally, I had to ask Jack, Ed, and Myrna Rae to take me to the clinic in a nearby town. Jack was fuming.

At the clinic, the doctor and the nurses confirmed what I had feared; another concussion – #2. Then they took me aside, away from Jack, and tried to convince me to press charges against Jack. They knew that the bruises on my wrists, arms, and shoulders were not part of the cuts and bruises on my face and head. Like the idiot and coward that I was, I denied it. What else could I do? I was alone and a long ways from home. To survive, I had to play the game and get along. And I had the sad, sick thought that, maybe, if I were good and loving, that this sort of thing would never happen again. So sad. What is even sadder is that I thought that if Jack wasn't punching and smacking me, it all wasn't really abuse. How could a grown, educated person be so uninformed and naive?

*****

Now, let me indulge myself with a whine-fest. At times I tried to hint to my girlfriends that something was wrong with my marriage, by telling them that Jack didn't treat me the way that I thought a husband should treat his wife. They all listened to what I was saying, but they did not hear what I was saying. It was not their fault, they didn't seem to understand what I was trying to say, and I was too embarrassed to elaborate. I figured that I was the problem. Now, looking back, I could kick myself for being a silly, weak, romantic fool who believed that love and kindness could cure anything. So, I forged ahead and tried very hard to make a go of the mess in which I was living. Although we still had some good times, they were becoming few and far between. Once we were married, it was as if I were being pushed to the background.

After our wedding, Jack, at age forty, moved from his parents' house (now, why didn't this raise a red flag?) into my cute little house (rental), but with no change in my routine or financial arrangement. Somehow, I was paying the rent and all of the bills with no help from my new hubby. Along with paying the bills, I cleaned, washed and ironed clothes, cooked every day, worked in the yard, entertained friends and family, helped him with his work, and taught school. To add injury to insult, believe it or not, the first ten years of our marriage, I took Jack breakfast in bed. That is, until one night in a drunken rage, he leaned into my face, spraying spit, and screamed that my fixing him breakfast every morning "didn't mean shit!" to him. Needless to say, he never got another breakfast in bed, even though he often wistfully hinted that it would be great if I started back.

Here is another anecdote that proves my point. One beautiful summer day, we went out in the boat for a day on the river with some of our friends – Jack's friend, William, and his wife, Elizabeth, and an old family friend, Madison. Elizabeth and I were sitting in lawn chairs in the back of the boat, and the men were standing and sitting under the canvas top, driving the boat and sipping liquor – lots of it. We were flying down the river – way too fast, way too careless, fueled by way too much alcohol. All of a sudden, the boat slammed to a stop; we had plowed into a sandbar. Everyone was thrown forward. The men were smushed up against the dashboard, Elizabeth was on the floor, and I was literally airborne, flying from the back towards the front. My flight was stopped when I smashed, face first, into the supporting rods of the canopy. My nose and lips were completely numb. It felt as if I had had a shot of Novocain to my face. To this day, Jack has yet to ask if I was alright. Instead, during the ensuing chaos, I quietly turned to Elizabeth, and asked, in a whisper, if my lip was bleeding. How Jack heard me, I don't know, but he did. He wheeled around and shouted for me to "Shut the f**k up!", and accused me of trying to get attention and make him look bad. His friend, Madison, in a shocked, almost angry, voice defended me, saying, 'Damn, Jack! You shut the f**k up! That girl just took a helluva lick without even a whimper! Leave her alone!' All I could think was "Thank you,

Madison," and why in the world am I with this man? Who was this pitiful, pathetic person I had become?

My mother always told us to try to always be kind, but to be very careful, because there are some people who mistake kindness as weakness. She told us to always draw a line in the sand and to never let anyone back us past that line. I must have forgotten to draw my line. Or maybe I set the line too far back.

*****

Looking back now, I, too, am baffled as to why I married a man who seemingly had absolutely no respect for me. But in my defense, in the beginning, I was completely wild about him, crazy in love with him, and in love with love. I thought that, if I loved him good enough and hard enough, I could save him, and he would change. But people don't change, not really, maybe superficially, but not deep down inside, inside the soul. So many people tried to talk me out of the marriage – obviously, they could see what I couldn't or wouldn't. Several of my grandmother's friends took me out to dinner and tried to reason with me. But you know how that goes; when you have a weakness for bad boys, and people bad-mouth them, it makes those boys all the more attractive, completely irresistible – wildly romantic, like Romeo and Juliet. Then one of my mother's dear friends took me aside and warned me to be careful because Jack was a "rounder." She might as well have poured catnip over him. She had made him absolutely irresistible. The warnings came from everywhere. Some do-gooders actually told me that Jack would never marry me because I wasn't his type. I am assuming they meant that I was too nice or too naive or too good for him, because we all know that cute is everybody's type. Then there were some naysayers who said that financially, since I wasn't an heiress, I wasn't his family's type. The nerve of some people! They might as well have thrown down a gauntlet. Did I mention that I was stubborn and hardheaded?

Some of what these people were saying must have gotten through, because strangely enough, on my wedding day, I had terrible misgivings and wanted to back out. But it was too late. What would I do? Where would I go? The three days prior to the wedding, Jack stayed completely inebriated, cavorting with his band of groomsmen, oblivious as to where I was or how I was. But I had already made my bed, and how could I possibly waste all that money that had already been spent on the big day. After all, things couldn't get much worse, right? Things could only get better, right?

*****

Dear me, this is the hardest and most distasteful part of my sad saga, but even though it is intimate, it must be told, because it is a huge part of the abuse in my marriage. I could skip over it, but it would not be fair to others who, like me, may not know that if a sex act causes one to feel uncomfortable, frightened, dirty, or in pain, it could very well be a form of sexual abuse. Plus, if I skip this part, then I am not being brave, or honest. If any words or actions do not feel right, then put a stop to it. Never be a chicken-livered wimp like me and endure what feels wrong or is wrong.

I will keep this brief. Jack was skilled in the act of lovemaking, but he was lousy at making love. He was very knowledgeable about the physical aspects of sex, but he was not when it came to the most important part: intimacy, "cuddling," talking. What came after sex, for him, was getting back to business as usual – a quick cleanup, fix a drink, and resume whatever he had been doing beforehand. Although I was not a virgin when we met (Hey! I grew up in the 70s, cut me some slack!), he made me feel like a clumsy amateur. I was always willing and compliant, at first, but I was unsure and uncomfortable with his moves and positions. He was rough, and many of his sexual preferences were uncomfortable, unnatural, and painful. When I finally got up the gumption to say no, he became very angry and vengeful. As far as I was concerned, anal and doggystyle were neither respectful nor normal – nor pleasant. I did not like it one bit. But if and when I said no, he would sit on top of me and try to force himself into my mouth; if I still said no, he would slap my face with his "member," thinking that would change my mind.

Often, during normal sex, he would grab me by my legs and yank me around the bed until he was positioned so that he could brace himself and ram as hard as possible. Or he would grab my legs and push them forward towards my shoulders. It hurt. I began to dread our "intimate" sessions. It was almost a relief when he began to have problems with erectile dysfunction. Four packs of cigarettes a day may have contributed to that. But don't worry, he was unstoppable. He began to use devices that helped him, but were terribly uncomfortable for me.

He constantly forced me to perform my "wifely duties," as he liked to call it, whenever or wherever he felt like having sex. He would try to have sex with me when I was asleep and even when I was sick. He never said that he loved me, instead, he complained and compared me to old girlfriends. He would often tell me, after sex, that I didn't know how to please a man, and would again compare me to old girlfriends. He made me feel unlovable and undesirable. It was a terrible secret to keep, embarrassing and humiliating. It was all about being groped in the kitchen, assaulted in the shower, and fingered in the car.

Most important of all, everyone knows it's all about kisses. Kissing is the most important element in the beginning and growth of a romance and relationship. Most disconcerting to me was the fact that when we kissed, Jack never closed his eyes. Well, you might say, you obviously didn't either. I did! But I would peek – everybody does. His eyes would be wide open, not looking at me, but looking around, almost like he was whistling and biding his time. There was so much more unhappiness and abuse, but enough said, it is a dark picture, and makes me sad to think about it, and embarrassed. I can't imagine how you must feel.

*****

Words… Words have limitless power and influence. Words can change the world, particularly your world. Anyone who thinks that only sticks and stones can hurt someone is sadly mistaken. Words have more impact and consequence than any handheld weapon. Words can erode, destroy, crush, humiliate, alienate, debase, annihilate, incite, and demoralize without striking a blow. How the words are delivered, the tone, can increase the power or damage of words exponentially.

Maybe to understand the thread I am pursuing, you should be aware of the spirit, the essence, of me that began to disappear as physical, sexual, and, probably most significantly, verbal and emotional abuse began to become the norm of our lives. I had always had a kind, gentle soul, a big heart, and a joyous, exuberant spirit. Some people are described as being an old soul. Not me. I was definitely a young soul: all optimism, enthusiasm, and laughter, with no worldly cynicism. Mama always told us to never be a "poor, poor, pitiful me" type of person; if something was bad or sad, to not cry or complain, but, instead, to find something funny about it and laugh. And we did! My sisters and I entertained ourselves endlessly. Some days were spent reading books, others were spent putting on plays, choreographing dance routines, and reading books and plays aloud with silly voices. We rode horses, swam, explored, and had a glorious childhood. We did everything together, with me cast as the family clown. I loved to make people smile and laugh.

For example, whenever we were at the town's public pool, I would get up to dive, and would make a huge production of readying myself, stretching and bouncing until I had all eyes on me. Then I would leap out and complete the biggest bellyflop ever, on purpose. If my sisters were shrieking with laughter, my mission was accomplished. And it was another good day. So, "bad" words and actions can diminish and almost destroy the essence and identity of a spirit, even an enthusiastic, exuberant, happy one. When Jack began to constantly criticize, belittle, berate, and ridicule me, what made me, me, began to slip away, until one day, I didn't recognize myself, and I couldn't find me anymore.

Chapter Three

If you were to see Jack and me together at a social function, you would think, like most people, that we were a perfect couple. Jack was lean, muscular, handsome, and larger-than-life. I was, and am, petite and slim, with dark curly hair – naturally curly! (A dear friend told me that I had to add charming to my description). We often went to nice parties, dances, and dinners, and had fun, cute friends. We actually had plenty of happy, fun times together in the beginning. After our first year of marriage, we moved into Jack's mother's beautiful house so that we could help take care of his widowed, ailing mother. She suffered from dementia. Along with some truly wonderful sitters, I helped take care of Mrs. M until her death, after which, we continued to live in the house. So, here we were, an attractive couple, a beautiful home, great friends. How could our lives not be perfect?

We had all the ingredients for success. So, what happened? Early on, the good times outweighed the bad, but sadly, life is unstoppable, and as life moved forward and onward, the fun times and days of contentment became distant memories. If Jack could keep his scotch consumption to five or six neat drinks, it would be a good day. But more and more often, the normal became ten to fifteen drinks, and it would be a very bad day. I did not know how to control or divert the dark days that were insidiously creeping into our lives, destroying our relationship with each other and our friends. My life was beginning to spin away from me, but no one seemed to suspect the chaos that had begun to define our life behind solid, closed, locked doors.

*****

I don't think Jack started out wanting to wound me with his words; I think his cruel, insulting words sprang from anger and frustration with himself. His feelings had to go somewhere, and he aimed them towards me – probably because I always foolishly took it and stayed. Maybe he thought that bringing me down would bolster and buoy him up. But it only made him sink lower, while dragging me down with him. Jack's verbal attacks began, every so often, early in our relationship, and seemed to usually spring from jealousy. Jealousy of my friends and anyone from my past. Sadly, having a jealous boyfriend can be a little exciting and romantic to a silly, lovestruck fool like me. At least, at first. Unfortunately, these attacks began to worsen and to increase in cruelty and frequency. In the beginning, when these attacks began, I was still my sassy self, and would take up for myself, which resulted in many an argument and nasty fight. After these fights, I would swear that I'd never speak to him again. But I always did. He would show up the next day, handsome, charming, acting as if nothing could possibly be wrong. It was as if I were under a spell, I would go right back to him until the next time, and there was always a next time.

Don't worry, I would never subject you to an endless play-by-play rendition of our seemingly endless sad saga. As I mentioned a while back, most of Jack's name-calling, at first, was of the "p***y-peddling whore" genre, along with crude, lewd references to my "snatch." Most of his diatribes were accusations concerning me and a ridiculous lineup of men, most of whom I didn't know, and none of whom I had ever dated. I used to tell Jack that he was the only person in the world who thought that I was some kind of femme fatale. He became suspicious and controlling, constantly trying to separate me from my friends. His suspicious, accusatory attitude made me become cautious, hesitant, submissive, and reserved.

As the years passed, and the alcohol consumption increased and intensified, the words became more of the "motherf*****g" and "f*****g" variety. Early on, I would sass him back and then flounce off to the bedroom, lock the door, and get on the bed to watch television or read a book. However, after the third door had been kicked open, I stopped locking the door. One, it was obviously fruitless, two, it was expensive, and three, it was too embarrassing to face the concerned, pitying looks from the workmen who fixed the doors. I was embarrassed and ashamed of myself, and ashamed for Jack. And once Jack broke through the door, he would loose all hell on me. Eventually, my survival instincts kicked in, and I became like any animal that has been mistreated on a regular basis; I learned to remain quiet and still, to lower my head and study the floor, to not make eye contact, and to try to virtually disappear, while praying that he would stop and go away.

As the tirades began to intensify, Jack began to stand over me, circling, while berating, deriding, and bullying me. His words? Everything had "stupid f****g" in front of it. I was a stupid f****g imbecile, a stupid f****g moron, a stupid f****g idiot, whore, and bitch. One of his favorite tactics was to let me escape to the upstairs so that he could stand at the foot of the stairs and shout up to me his favorite insult. It was a line from the John Grisham book, *The Rainmaker;* "You must be STUPID, STUPID, STUPID!"

I had become proficient at reading Jack's level of drunkenness and frame of mind. Often, I could tell that he was going to pass out shortly, so I would remain quietly seated until he did, and then I would slip away. Sometimes, I could sense his mood changing in time for me to discreetly go on up to bed before he became argumentative; all the while, I would pray that he would stay downstairs and pass out. The nights that he didn't, I could hear him coming up the stairs, and my heart would shrink. I would often try to pretend that I was asleep, but it was usually futile. He would stumble into the room, approaching the bed, muttering to himself. Then he would grasp the covers and strip them off the bed, then crawl from the foot of the bed up to me until he was in my face. Then he would say or do any number of unpleasant things.

Sometimes, I would forget to pay attention to the number of drinks being consumed or to any changes in his tone of voice or demeanor, usually because I was reading or was engrossed in a movie. But the dogs wouldn't be distracted. They could always hear the change in his voice.

35

When this would happen, the two larger dogs would quickly get up and run upstairs, and then the small dog would start anxiously scratching at my legs, whining, begging to get in the chair with me. Whenever this happened, my heart and breathing would stop, my stomach would flip, and I would feel cold and clammy, because I knew, without a doubt, that Jack was coming after me.

Then one day, I had an absolute brainstorm, a way to help both of us, a way to help Jack understand what he was doing and saying to me, and to help our floundering marriage. I thought that if Jack could hear what he was saying when he was drunk, and how he was saying it, he would straighten up and be the good man that I knew was still somewhere inside of him. So, I told Jack that I was going to buy a small digital recorder, and explained that I was going to record some of his drunken ramblings and tantrums, so that he could listen later and understand what was happening. Well, I am sure that you know how that went over. Oh, well, the best-laid plans. I bought the recorder anyway. When an attack would begin, I would hold up the recorder for him to see, and then I would set it on the table next to me, and let it record the night's activities. Naturally, Jack refused to ever listen to the tapes. For about two years, I would intermittently tape our "sessions," and then would usually eventually erase them. Until, one day I stopped erasing.

Unsurprisingly, the frequency and fury of the tirades were escalating. One night, against my better judgment, Jack and I went to a local bar and grill for St. Patrick's Day. Jack must have thought it was time to go "public." I was standing near the bar, chatting with a friend, when I saw my friend glance, startled, in Jack's direction. I quickly turned to look and saw Jack towering over someone, talking excitedly in his face. All I needed to see was Jack's posture, and I knew, I knew that all hell was about to break loose. I rushed over, got between the two men, and pushed Jack away. Then I grabbed him by the arm and began to steer him out the door, and across the street to where we had parked. When we got to the car, I tried to get Jack into the passenger-side door. He pulled away and grabbed me by my shoulders and threw me back against the car parked next to us. He loomed over me, scowling, and began to curse and swear at me, accusing me of embarrassing him in the bar. As he shouted, he thumped me repeatedly on the chest as an emphasis to his words. I did not know how this was going to end. Then, suddenly, a voice! A man, a lawyer, in fact, had walked out of the bar to smoke a cigarette, and had heard and then seen what was going on across the street. He crossed the street, saying, 'Hey! What's going on here?' Jack quickly stepped away from me, and I leaped forward, trying to push him into the car, while thanking our friend and begging him to not call the police. I explained that I was taking Jack home immediately. We returned home safely, but not happily.

That night was one of the last nights that I went to a bar, a dance, or a large party that wasn't family-oriented. I had had enough. It also marked the day that I stopped erasing the tapes. The tirades had become meaner and nastier day by day, decency no longer a factor, and all documented on tape. By now, he was accusing me of f****g every man in town, f****g his brothers, and sickest of all, f****g my dogs. I knew that I could not keep living like this, but I didn't know what to do, or how to do it. I was scared. I was alone. And what about my animals? Where could I go, and take them? I felt trapped with no way out.

Finally, out of desperation, I approached Jack's brothers, separately, and asked them to help me get Jack into rehab and anger management, and both of us into marriage counseling. Later, that day, Ed came by the house, sent me out to the porch, and talked to Jack. My God, I was so relieved, I almost cried. After Ed left, Jack asked me if I wanted to know what Ed had to say.

I replied with, "Of course!"

"Well," he said with a smirk, "he said that I have a whiney wife, and that the next time we had a fight, to keep it to ourselves."

Wow, I really was all alone. I felt trapped, frozen, diminished. After that day, on the nights when Jack crawled up the bed to me, he would pin me against the headboard with his hand around my throat and would threaten to break my neck with one squeeze of his hand. Some nights, he would hold me down on the bed and would stuff trash in my face, ordering me to "Eat it! Breathe it!" All the while, my trusty little tape recorder lay on the bedside table, recording away. And he thought that I was the stupid one!

Chapter Four

Now, I feel that I have to address what is probably the most tragic aspect of our doomed relationship: the unrelenting grasp of alcoholism on Jack. Alcoholism ran rampant in his family, and everything they did seemed to center around alcohol consumption. Over the years, I watched a vibrant, beautiful man, who had a good heart, and a zest for everything fun in life, become a meanspirited, sour, bitter drunk, who blamed all his problems on others, especially me. In the beginning, we, with our friends, partied very hard and drank way too much into the wee hours of the morning. Jack was the life of every party. He reveled in partying, dancing, laughing, cutting up, and being wild and crazy. Ahhh…youth!

As time marched onward, as it has a tendency to do, most of us mellowed somewhat as we got older; fewer drinks, earlier to bed, more responsible. But not Jack. So, I became his keeper. I became his designated driver. His enabler. I spent the majority of my time trying to drag him out of bars and parties before he became obnoxious, antagonistic, or made a fool of himself.

Once I got him home, I could usually manage to get him from the car to the house, although maneuvering him up the stairs was unbelievably tough. Sometimes, he would fall flat in the yard, and I would be hard-pressed to get him up and going, but I am exceedingly determined. Some nights when he passed out in the car before I could make it home, I would have to just give up, put a blanket over him, and let him sleep it off in the car. When drunk at home, Jack would careen around the house, stumbling and falling, breaking windows, chairs, small tables, glasses, and mirrors. Not to mention that he hurt himself, cuts, separated shoulders, and bumps on his head. I was scared for his life, and mine. Through the years, he also managed to alienate many of our friends.

Sometimes, as we were driving down a highway, he would open the car door and lean out – sometimes as we were traveling in excess of 75 miles per hour, in heavy traffic. He was usually looking for a cigarette he had dropped. Several times, I had to hold his shirt and drive with one hand, trying to get to the side of the road so that I could reel him in. Thankfully, some of the other times, friends who were with us, would hold onto him until I could somehow get to the side of the road. Pretty heart-stopping! Strangely enough, he was always furious at me after these incidents.

Some nights, I would get calls from bartenders, at two or three in the morning, saying that Jack was in their bar, and was too drunk to drive. I would crawl out of bed, pull on clothes over my pajamas, and go get him. It was embarrassing. But to be honest, if Jack were to win an award for World's Worst Drunk, I should win for World's Biggest Enabler. Sadly, I never figured out what exactly to do to help him. Talking to or fussing with him just made him worse. His parents and his brothers seemed to shrug it off as my problem, and Jack refused to go to any kind of program or counseling. So, I was left with no alternative but to watch the man I loved disappear into the sinister, all-consuming grasp of another lover: his addiction to alcohol. I had to watch the life I had dreamed of disintegrate. The culmination of it all occurred during The Weekend. From that point on, my life was an avalanche of changes and emotions – unstoppable and irreversible.

*****

So, we are about to enter a huge maelstrom precipitated by what we, my friends and I, refer to as The Weekend. It is the pivotal weekend that heralded the impending storm. Before we journey into The Weekend, I feel that I need to explain why I didn't pack up and leave at the first signs of abuse, why I stayed with a charismatic, but insufferable, bully.

Lame Excuse:
#1. Suffering quietly and proudly is the Southern way. In many parts of the South, particularly the rural areas, it is still a man's world. Husbands rule the roost and do pretty much anything and anyone they please, while the wife, like a second class citizen, keeps the home fires burning and the family intact, while also keeping her mouth shut. Divorce, in the nicer circles, is very frowned upon and scandalous. I thought we were in the 21st century.

#2. I truly loved Jack, and I understood him better than he sometimes understood himself. I recognized that he was abused, neglected, and damaged as a child by his family, particularly his scurrilous brothers. As you know, since I am Jesus Christ of the Animal World, I thought it my duty and moral responsibility to try to help the wounded creature inside Jack's soul. I foolishly and stubbornly thought that constant, unremitting love, understanding, and loyalty would somehow eradicate the need to strike out and hurt and belittle.

#3. If I left Jack, I would have nowhere to go. My parents were dead, my siblings had moved away. I had no one on my side, no one to help me. I felt completely alone.

#4. I was not financially independent. I would be starting over with absolutely nothing on which to live. I had always funneled my money into paying bills and keeping the house and grounds up to par. I was scared, no, I was terrified.

#5. One of the most significant factors: my pets. They were my friends and my solace. I could never betray their trust, loyalty, and love by leaving them behind. Where could I go? Who would rent to someone with animals? I could not afford to buy a house. I had to stay so that I could be with them.

#6. Jack used to threaten me with the promise that, if I ever tried to leave him, he would make sure that I would be living in a single-wide trailer, in the middle of a field, with no money, and no friends. I believed him, and the thought of that bleak future was absolutely and totally paralyzing.

#7. I was alone and scared.

8. I was afraid people would think we were trashy.

#9. I didn't want people to dislike Jack. Pathetic, right?

#10. I had to survive.

*****

When I began, out of desperation, to try to tell someone about the hurtful, shameful life that was mine, I did not know how to broach the subject. I was unsure as to how people would react. I was ashamed of my life and of myself for letting my life become such a miserable mess. As I mentioned before, I had been regaling my friends with tales of my and Jack's escapades, keeping it light and fun. I was always Jack's biggest and best cheerleader. Sometimes, though, I would test the waters by inserting a small, unsavory "nugget" into the story, in the hopes that someone would pick up on it. But no one ever did. They were all too entertained listening to my stories, and didn't hear what I was subtly trying to express. It was the reverse of the old saying that you can't see the forest for the trees; they were seeing the forest, but I wanted them to see the trees.

Then one day, an avenging angel named Annie strode into my life. She was beautiful, generous, and no-nonsense. Maybe it was because she was new to town and didn't have old relationships clouding her vision, but Annie listened to me. And oh frabjous day, she heard me. She refused to listen to, or accept, any excuses for Jack's bad behavior. Tall, slim, and fearless, she was like a combination of Joan of Arc, Xena the Princess Warrior, and Wonder Woman. She was my hero, my friend, my savior, and my first ray of hope that maybe, just maybe, there was a way out of this incredibly sordid mess. As I began to finally confide in her, it was becoming frighteningly and terrifyingly apparent that my life with Jack had become toxic and dangerous.

43

It was clear that something had to be done. Annie's outrage was like a tonic to me. She made me see that I wasn't the problem, that I wasn't to blame, and that I was in danger and needed to get out – immediately. I can't begin to describe the feeling of relief that flooded through me just knowing that I wasn't crazy. But still, I stalled. I couldn't make the move. The thought of freedom was overwhelming and terrifying. I was like a caged animal that has been imprisoned so long that when the door is finally swung open, it refuses to go.

Annie's strength created a small spark of hope that ignited inside of me. It would take a long time to burst into flames, but it was there, warming in the ashes. Annie was concerned and frightened for my life. I was so tempted, so very tempted, to break free, and then, I would lose my nerve and stay. Then, one day, God must have seen all that He could stand and said, "Enough!" because The Weekend happened. From then on, my life, as it was, began to scatter and blow away like leaves in a storm. In the midst of this, Annie had helped me find my line in the sand.

Ahhh... The Weekend. What a holy mess! What an unholy mess! That weekend I watched as Jack reeled about drunkenly, insulting friends, coming apart. All veneers and facades were stripped away. He revealed to everyone the ugly side he usually saved for me. And there was nothing I could do. The cat was not just out of the bag, it had ripped its way out, yowling and tearing, nasty and vicious. There was no way conceivable to hide, diffuse, or halt the raging storm. I could only watch, aghast, horrified, embarrassed, and so, so sad. I was ashamed and full of sorrow for me and for Jack. I watched in horror as this once charming man, staggering about, stripped away all the years of my shielding, protecting, and covering up his very dark side. I was way beyond ashamed and way beyond humiliated. Now, everyone knew the dark side of Jack, and the secretive, weak, pitiable side of me.

So, I imagine that now you are very curious about The Weekend. Fix a drink and settle in, I will spin you a sad tale!

*****

Let me begin by, as usual, defending Jack, and saying that he was not all to blame. I actually had a hand in this mess, but was not prepared for what all transpired. My birthday was coming up, and my sister, a friend, and I thought it would be fun to celebrate at the beach house with a very small crowd, no big party. Jack, who was always up for an opportunity to party, seemed strangely ambivalent, but didn't object. Since the beach was less than an hour away, my sister (who had recently moved back) and I decided that, instead of paying someone to care for my animals and her cats, we would take turns driving home and back, from the beach, to feed and check on the animals. So, the weekend was planned! My sister, Jack, and I were to drive to the beach Friday evening to open up the house, and our guests, all three of them, would arrive sometime Saturday. I had invited one of my dearest, childhood friends, Bette, who loved, loved, loved the beach, and a nice couple whom Jack and I both liked. The wife was a lawyer and worlds of fun, and her husband was a government official, loved to fish and often took Jack fishing with him. Then Jack called another couple who had their own house at the beach. They were pleased and said that they were going to be at their beach house anyway. It sounded like a perfect birthday weekend. Everything was planned. Then, it began to fall apart.

Suddenly, on Thursday, my sister announced that she was going to visit our brother in Florida instead of going to the beach. I was cool with that, but it left me with the dilemma of caring for both her pets and mine by myself. Then Friday blew in, literally. It was a rainy, windy, stormy day. When I got home from work at 6:30, the rain was coming down in buckets. The dogs refused to go out, and I certainly didn't blame them. The problem was that I couldn't leave until they had attended to their business, and had eaten. Jack was restless, and curiously agitated and angry. By 9:30, the rain had not let up at all. So, I told Jack that I thought that we should wait and go to the beach early in the morning. None of our house guests were expected until lunchtime Saturday. Jack went ballistic! He started shouting, "What about the Wrights? They are already at the beach! They think that we are coming tonight!"

I looked at him, and reminded him that they were in their own house, and not dependent on us for a place to stay. And it was already getting late. I said that we could just call them and tell them we were not coming until tomorrow morning because of the storm. There was no way that they could blame us or be angry. Jack began to rant and rave, slamming around the house in a complete rage. I told him that he could go ahead and drive to the beach if he wanted to brave the storm, but that I would have to come early in the morning after I had taken care of all of the pets. It made no sense, this late at night, to drive to the beach and then have to turn around and come back at five in the morning to take care of them again. Jack was adamant that he had to go to the beach that night. So, I put on my rain gear and loaded his car with sheets, towels, toilet paper, paper towels, soap, and coffee, and promised to be at the beach by 9:00 in the morning. He slammed out of the house and roared away, but not before nastily insinuating that I must have "other plans."

The rain had slowed to a drizzle the next morning, and I was as good as my word. I pulled onto the beach and up to our house at 8:45 in the morning. The house was locked and dark. There was no car at the house, and no one in the house, and I did not have a key. Well, thank goodness for a cell phone. I called Jack's number, and miracle of miracles, he actually answered. He had spent the night at the Wrights' house, and had not even bothered to come by our house. Well, I am sorry to say that I was a little fussy, and asked him to come let me into the house. I then fussed about the fact that he had not opened up the house or unloaded his car. I was, unknowingly, setting the stage for a world of unpleasantness.

When he made it to the house, I fussed some more for a few minutes, just fussy, not anything horrible. When he became belligerent and threatening, I realized that I was on the verge of ruining the day, and had to save it. So, I stopped, took a deep breath, and said, 'Jack, I'm sorry. I'm being a bitch. Let's start over. Just stop, and let's go for a walk on the beach. Relax. Then come back and just start over. Fresh.' Well, he did walk on the beach with me. Cold, scary, barely suppressing his anger. When we got back to the house, I thought that maybe things were a little better. Not great, but better, and would be fine. So, I unloaded the cars, put away the groceries, made the beds, put out towels and soap, and fixed lunch. Jack refused to eat. Then he left without telling me where he was going. I was at the beach house alone until our guests arrived. They brought laughter, warmth, and a sense of fun to a lonely house and what had been a pretty depressing day. It looked like things were finally looking up.

Jack, very rudely, didn't come back to the house for hours. Around 5:00, I made sure everyone was fine, and then drove back to town to take care of animals. When I returned around 7:30, my heart sank as I walked into the house. Jack was home, in style! He was reeling drunkenly around the house, loudly making odd remarks, and talking excitedly into everyone's face. He had a crazed, furious scowl on his face that was unsettling, at least, to me, because I knew what it could portend. I spoke to everyone and went into the bedroom to change so that I could help fix supper. I heard Jack come into the bedroom. He pinned me against the wall, and snarling, he accused me of going back to town to meet someone. Then he began to rage at me for inviting people he didn't "give a shit about." I was speechless. These were all good friends whom we had always enjoyed. I slipped from his grasp and hurried out of the room to thankfully join my friends. There really is safety in numbers!

Unexpectedly, some people from our town, who also had beach houses, showed up to visit. They had been driving around, and had seen the lights on in our house and the cars in the drive, and thought they'd pop in, say hello, and have a little libation. Jack went postal. He collared me in the kitchen and backed me up against the kitchen counter.

In a sinister, creepy, strangely nasal voice, he said, 'I thought you weren't inviting a lot of people! You must think you are cute, inviting all these people I don't even like!'

He was going to say more, but a friend walked up behind him, saying, 'Hey! Hey! Hey! What's going on? Lighten up!' I broke free, and Jack staggered off. I thanked the friend, tried to cover for Jack's bad behavior, and nervously went back to trying to be a gracious hostess.

People were looking at me with raised, questioning eyebrows, some with outstretched hands along with alarmed expressions, and others mouthing words like "What's with him?", "What's going on?", and "Are you okay?" All I could do was smile and shrug, I wanted to cry.

By this time, Jack had collapsed on the sofa, and was excitedly talking, loudly and closely, to one of our friends with whom he had spent Friday night. My friend, Bette, looked at me and signaled that she was going over to try to calm Jack down. He was talking wildly, slurring his words, bobbing and weaving on the sofa, and using foul language. Not long after Bette had sat down next to him, he suddenly leaped up, grabbed a bottle of whiskey, staggered to the bedroom, and slammed and locked the door.

I was horribly embarrassed, but almost weak with relief that he was gone for a while. Unbelievably and happily, he stayed away for several hours, and we all actually relaxed and had a nice time. Every now and then, I would listen at the bedroom door. I could hear muttering and cursing, and some bumps and crashes. As the night wore on, everyone except the house guests left. Suddenly, Jack wrenched the bedroom door open, and drunkenly staggered out in his underwear. He had a cut on his forehead. He advanced towards us, and we scattered like a frightened flock of chickens. I slipped into the bedroom and grabbed my toothbrush and my hairbrush, and hid them in the powder room. Meanwhile, Jack grabbed another bottle of Scotch and staggered back to the bedroom, and once again slammed and locked the door.

I, futilely, tried to make everyone think that everything was fine, and that Jack was just exhausted from a long, hard week at work, and had had too much to drink, obviously! No one looked as if he or she believed anything I was saying. I had to sit up until everyone finally went to bed, which was very late, so that I could sleep on the sofa. I was too embarrassed to let them know that I was completely locked out of the bedroom. I slept for a few hours, then had to get up and drive home to feed pets. While I was home, I also showered and changed, and then drove back to the beach. I got back right around 9:00. Jack had not emerged from his lair, so all was quiet and peaceful. Our friends came downstairs around 10:30. We fixed some coffee, and then went down on the beach, mainly so we could safely talk about what the devil was going on with Jack. When we walked back up to the house, Jack was gone, his clothes were gone, and his car was gone. The bedroom was a mess.

Not knowing what else to do, or where Jack had disappeared to, we decided to fix a brunch and pack up and leave after we ate and cleaned up the house. Just as we were packing up, Jack appeared, walking in with a friendly, pleasant smile. I was completely flabbergasted and bewildered. So was everybody else. I knew, in my heart, that this was a strange calm before a very big storm. At least, we ended the weekend on a pleasant note, and everybody headed home. Not much of a birthday weekend!

Since Jack and I had both of our cars at the beach, we drove home and arrived home separately. I was apprehensive and a little frightened because I didn't know what was waiting for me, or what was going to happen to me when I entered the house. For the first time in several days, we were going to be completely alone with each other. Nothing happened! I couldn't believe it, but I was not going to let my guard down. Jack was uncharacteristically quiet. It was almost as if he were giving me the silent treatment, but I was happy with anything that wasn't cruel or violent. We remained in the eerie, gothic, strange super-quiet atmosphere for about two days, and then our life began to fall apart, bit by bit, faster and faster. I guess God had decided that He had to speed things along since He had helped start this mess. The end came like a landslide, but I had finally had enough. I was tired of running and hiding. I was tired of being afraid, tired of being ashamed, tired of trying to control the beast within Jack. The time had come for me to stand my ground, on my line in the sand, come what may – and it came with a vengeance.

Chapter Five

Now, onto the aftermath of The Weekend. For the first three days after The Weekend, Jack and I lived in an almost silent, subzero climate. It actually suited me fine – except I was waiting for whatever I knew must be coming. It was. It did. On the evening of the third day. I can't even remember what triggered it all. I think it might have been because I had gone over to a friend's house for iced coffee without Jack's permission. Who knows? It didn't have to be anything that made sense. All that I remember clearly is that I was in the den, standing by the arm of a large leather chair, asking Jack a question about something mundane like supper or laundry. He rose angrily from his chair and moved towards me until he was directly across from me. He said something to me, but it didn't register because I was transfixed by the fury on his face. But then he said: "You. Stupid. F*****g. C**T!" I felt my mouth literally drop open. I couldn't breathe. He had called me every name in the book, but he had never called me the "C" word. Until today. It is, without a doubt, the most vile, loathsome word ever conceived or spoken. That moment was the straw, as in the legendary straw that broke the camel's back. I stood for a moment, stupefied, breathless, and I knew, in my heart, that I was through with this man. Done. Finished. I didn't know how or when I could get away from him, but it was coming. I no longer had any desire to be with this man, and certainly not for the rest of my life. All I could think about was, here I am, already older, with a mean, drunken, disrespectful husband; I refuse to be eighty-plus years old, still with an old, crazed, drunken husband who is still calling me shameful, denigrating, belittling names.

When I went upstairs that night, I lay in the bed, trying to read a book, but all I could think about was my seemingly hopeless, miserable situation. Then, horror of horrors, I heard him coming up the stairs, muttering, definitely drunk. He threw the door open and staggered towards the bed. Pulling the covers off, he crawled up to me and put his hands around my neck. I don't know where it came from, but I heard my voice, strong and clear, tell him to take his hands off of me. And he did! He backed off, crashed around the room, cursing for a while, then collapsed on the bed, and passed out. The next day, I moved into the downstairs guest bedroom (something I often did), and we resumed our icy, gothic life, going through all the motions with cool civility.

A few days later, on a Saturday afternoon, my sister and my friends Bette and Rhett came over. It had been one week since The Weekend. This was the first chance we had had to get together to dissect and discuss Jack's bizarre behavior at the beach. Jack had gone somewhere, he didn't tell me where, and I didn't care, but we had the house to ourselves. We sat on the front porch, sipping wine, and tried to make sense of Jack's meltdown. Bette had been there, but the other two had not. Bette kept repeating, 'Oh, my God, I have never seen him act like that! He acted like he was out of his mind! It was like Dr. Jekyll and Mr. Hyde! He must have been on drugs or something!' We dissected and discussed it, then hashed and rehashed it.

Then, Bette gave me an odd look, and with a huge sigh, said, 'I have been wrestling with myself about whether or not I should tell you something.'

We all jumped like we had been hit with a cattle prod. 'Of course, you have to tell us! There is no way that you can leave us hanging after saying something like that!'

So, reluctantly, Bette began her revelation. She said that, that night at the beach, when she had sat down next to Jack to try to calm him down, that he had said something very strange. (She definitely had our undivided attention!) Then, she said that, while they were talking, Jack's cell phone had been lying on the coffee table in front of him. He picked it up and put it in his pocket, and began patting it, saying, 'Oh, my! There are pictures. Easy to take. Hard to get rid of.' Over and over. Then he mumbled, incoherently, something about me, and that I mustn't find out.

I looked at Bette, jumped up, and ran into the house. I looked in the bowl Jack usually dropped his keys and phone into at night. I could hardly breathe. I was shaking. Unbelievable! The cell phone was there! He never – I mean never – left home without that phone. It was like a Divine Intervention, like it was meant to be. I had never looked at Jack's phone before, I had always respected his privacy. To hell with it! I grabbed the phone and dashed back to the porch. Cell phones were new to me, and my hands were shaking. We played around with it, with a sense of urgency. Scared to death Jack would drive up any minute.

Then, suddenly, I hit the right button. And saw something that no woman should ever have to see. Picture after picture, dozens of them. My husband had taken selfies of himself with a vagrant woman who was performing fellatio on him. We all gasped. Everyone shrieked, "Gross!" and looked away, except Rhett, who, true to form, reached over, took the phone and enlarged the pictures. I felt nauseous, almost like I had a huge rock in my stomach. Bette looked at me, sadness all over her face, and asked me if I was sure that it was Jack, and did I know who the woman was. Yes, and yes.

*****

Yes, of course it was Jack. It didn't matter how much or how little of him the pictures showed, after being together for over thirty years, I would recognize any part of him anywhere. And yes, I knew the woman. Her name was Glenda. She had had a sad life, and had been in and out of our lives since she was in college. Her mother had dated Jack's brother, Mark. After college, Glenda slipped into a world of drug addiction, alcoholism, mental illness, prostitution, and vagrancy. In fact, her mother broke up with Mark because she walked in on Mark and Glenda having sex. Glenda's family tried everything to pull her out of her life in a cesspool, but it was hopeless; she did not want to be helped.

Jack had given Glenda a part-time job in his office. He said that when she was sober and straight (which wasn't often), she did a good job. When she wasn't sober or straight, he said that he sent her home, or at least out of the office. Who knows if that was true? In Jack's defense, I do think that in the beginning, his heart was in the right place and that he was honestly trying to help her. Obviously, it all took a perverse and perverted turn for the worse.

It is almost laughable what a trusting idiot in denial I was, laughable but sad. I am going to recount two of the most telling episodes in my relationship with Glenda. Both incidents took place a little over a year before the discovery of the pictures. One cold, rainy day, my friend Rhett called me in distress. She was going to rent a house from a friend who was in a nursing home, with the stipulation that she care for his aged dog which was still living in the house. Rhett's friend had been paying a neighbor to look after his dog while he was in the nursing home; he kept thinking that he would be able to come home eventually. When Rhett went into the house, she discovered that the poor, old pug had been living in a 3' by 5' box for almost two years. The poor thing was in deplorable condition, completely covered in feces and urine, and barely able to walk – but still sweet and delighted to see Rhett. So, I, Jesus Christ of the Animal World, leaped into action and savior mode to take the poor creature to a groomer, a veterinarian, and then back to a clean bed and a decent life with Rhett.

I rarely went by Jack's office because I didn't want to be a nosey, pain-in-the-neck, interfering wife, and because he wasn't particularly nice to me when I did. Since he always wanted to know where I was, I thought that it would be easier for me to run in and tell him what I was doing. I knocked on his office door, and then walked in. There sat Glenda, at Jack's drafting table – naked, wrapped in a towel, sipping on a beer. I stood in the doorway, stupefied and speechless. Jack, red-faced, was fiercely and frantically slamming and banging the filing cabinet drawers. I guess he was stalling for time to think about what he was going to say to me and was distracting me with all the activity – as if he were doing office business and not monkey business. He walked towards me with his hands outstretched, spinning some story about how Glenda was having some troubles, that she and her alcoholic boyfriend were living in a tent, and that she needed somewhere to get cleaned up. So, he had let her shower at his office. He must have thought that I really was a fool. I coolly acted as if I believed his sorry lie. Glenda stayed where she was with a smirky smile on her face. I looked Jack in the face and told him what I had come to tell him, and then turned to Glenda and told her that I was sorry that she was having a hard time, bid them farewell and left.

Jack followed me to my car, and when we were out of earshot of his office, I looked him straight in the eye, pointed toward his office, and said, "That doesn't suit me! At all. I don't know what is going on, but I don't like it. Plus, what if I had been a client? You could lose all your business! Get rid of her!" I jumped into my car and left. He fired her for about a week, at least he said he did. She was right back at his office in no time.

A few weeks later, another incident took place. Jack and I were home one Saturday afternoon, getting dressed to go to some family function. I, as usual, was ready first, so I told Jack that I would go ahead and take the car to gas it up, and come back for him. I returned home, and as I walked into the hall, I could hear Jack still in the shower. I walked into the den and there sat Glenda, in my favorite chair, no less!

Totally surprised, I managed to stay cool and polite. I thanked Glenda for coming to visit, and told her that we were getting ready to go somewhere and didn't have time to visit. Instead of getting up and leaving, she continued to sit in my chair, and started telling me a sob story about how she didn't have anywhere to stay. Bear in mind that she had a mother, a sister, two aunts, an uncle, and countless cousins living in town who would gladly try to help her. I felt bad for her, if it was true, but I could not let her insert herself any further into our lives. So, even though it was out of character for me, I told her that she could not stay with us and that she needed to go so that we could go to our family do. She left. I watched, and have to admit that I felt a tug of pity.

When Jack came running downstairs, late as usual, he had the nerve to ask me where Glenda was, which let me know that he knew that she had been in the house. As we drove out of the yard, Jack crept along very slowly, looking for her, until he spotted her talking to one of our neighbors. He wanted to stop and check on her, but I told him no, and said that she was not welcome in our house, his office, or our lives. I know it was wishful thinking to expect him to listen to a mealy-mouthed coward like me, so, of course, he ignored my wishes.

So, yes, I knew her.

*****

Now, here we were, sitting on the porch, completely blown away by The Pictures. None of us were savvy enough to send the pictures to someone's phone or computer, so we decided to say nothing until we could come up with some kind of strategy. My poor brain was in a whirl, this was worse than I had imagined. Believe it or not, I did the exact opposite of what you think I would do. But there was some crazy kind of method to my madness. I did not say a word about the pictures to Jack. I needed to process everything, and to try to figure out what in the world I was going to do. First, I moved back into the master bedroom. I know that it sounds ludicrously crazy, but I kept thinking, rethinking, and overthinking the topsy-turvy dung heap of a mess I was in. I kept replaying in my mind all of the recent events, and kept trying to remember some of the odd things Jack had said to me lately.

He had said some odd things about how he was not going to leave his bedroom, but that he would run me out – and I was out. Suddenly, I was afraid that maybe he was going to throw me out and divorce me on the grounds that I had abandoned the marital bed and refused to carry out my wifely duties. It is amazing what crazy things come to mind when you are scared and distraught. If he threw me out now, I had no plan in place, and would be out on the street like a homeless person, like Glenda, and so would my pets. I looked the reality of divorce in the face, and I quailed. So, I crept back to our bedroom like a whipped puppy, and continued to endure the cold sham of a marriage that we had, while desperately trying to figure out what on God's green earth I was going to do.

*****

Believe it or not, deservedly or not, I still cared for Jack. There's just no controlling the heart. When we first met, the sight of him used to make me catch my breath, but my feelings were not like that anymore; nevertheless, I couldn't not care. However, he was like a poison that was slowly eating away at me, and destroying the essence of me. The next two weeks were relatively calm. Not peaceful, but quiet and cold, a strained, forced calm. We were outwardly cordial and coolly polite, but we weren't having any fun. In the old days, whenever I walked past Jack on my way to the kitchen or the hall, I would always ruffle his hair or touch his shoulder as I passed. I would always do thoughtful things for him like fix coffee, bring his meal in on a tray, any kind of favor. Well, definitely no more of that. I did just enough to keep tempers in check so that I could survive while I formed some kind of exit plan, if it came to that, and I was pretty sure that we were headed that way. Sooner rather than later. Then two weeks to the day of the discovery of The Pictures, the precarious foundation I had been balancing on began to fall apart.

*****

That pivotal morning, after I had made the coffee, and was cleaning up the kitchen, Jack, without looking up from the newspaper, announced that he needed to go to the mall (which was forty miles away) to get some lens papers for his glasses, and since he was going to the mall, the least he could do was take me to a movie. From his tone of voice, I was pretty sure that he didn't care if I went or not. Or maybe I am becoming a cynical old soul. I would like to think that he really wanted me to go to make up for what all had been going on, but more than likely, he probably just wanted to make sure that he took his designated driver along, just in case he wanted to have a few pops on the way home. He wanted to go to an early-afternoon movie, so I had several hours to run to the IGA to pick up some things, and then time to go to one of my favorite stores, the Dollar General.

As I came out of the Dollar General, I spotted Fiona, an old family friend, standing outside in front of her antique store. I had some time, so I strolled over to chat with her. I had, in the past, confided a little in her, telling her that marriage to Jack was not what I had expected. I told her what I had told my friends, that Jack did not treat me the way I thought a husband would treat his wife. I thought that she had acted unusually interested, but when she didn't follow through with anything, I let it go. As we were chatting, who should clomp up to the store across the street but my dear friend, Glenda. I must have had an odd look on my face, or stared for too long. Either way, Fiona asked me if something was wrong. I started to tell her that nothing was amiss, but something made me turn to her and tell her about The Pictures. Fiona straightened up until her back was like a ramrod, and said to me, 'Honey, go sit in my store and wait until these customers are gone. I have something to tell you that I should have told you fifteen or twenty years ago.'

I had a terrible sinking feeling that this was not going to be anything that I really wanted to hear. When the customers finally left, Fiona locked the door behind them, and turned to me, a sad but determined look on her face. Definitely not going to be any great news.

She said, 'I should have told you this years ago. Your husband has, and has had for over twenty years, a girlfriend that he takes care of and visits every day. Everybody in town knows about it. We all thought that you knew and just didn't care.'

I felt like someone had slugged me in the gut. I couldn't breathe. I felt small and frozen and diminished. Everything seemed to drain out of my body, except for a huge lump in my stomach. But, I believed her. Something deep inside of me had suspected, for a long time that something was terribly amiss in our relationship. I just didn't realize that something had been amiss our entire marriage. But it certainly made sense – little pieces of the crazy puzzle of our marriage suddenly fit. This would prove to be a huge illumination.

As Fiona began to describe the details of Jack's sordid affair, a light bulb went off in my muddled brain, and a swell of nausea followed. When Fiona asked if I wanted to know the woman's name, I held up a shaky hand to stop her, and said, 'No, let me tell you. Gladys Cootye.'

Fiona blinked in surprise, 'You are right! How did you know? Let me tell you, she is a nasty piece of work!'

Oh, yes, I knew all about what kind of person Gladys Cootye was. In fact, I knew all I wanted to know about her, but had the sinking feeling that I was going to hear a lot more. When Fiona called her a nasty piece of work, she wasn't telling me anything I didn't already know. I had thought that that filthy piece of trash was out of our lives for good. I should have known better. Gladys Cootye had worked in Jack's office before Jack and I were married, and a few years after our marriage. Good Lord! She wasn't even cute! She was short and dumpy, and looked like she had been ridden hard, beaten, whipped, spurred, and then put up hot! Or in layman's terms, she was a nasty, rough, redneck, trashy skank.

Undeniably, Gladys was a raging alcoholic, and shook and trembled all of the time. I often wondered why Jack kept her around the office. Now I knew, and I should have known. Although, I didn't particularly like Gladys, when I saw her at the office, true to form, I was always pleasant and kind, asking her about her son, commiserating with her about the woes of old cars, and I always wished her well for weekends and holidays. I guess she and Jack had some good laughs about what a foolish ninny I was. After a while, even I began to get some odd vibes off of her, but she stopped working for Jack before I could confront him. I did not know her circumstances, but she was living in the projects with her "boyfriend" and her son, and did not have a job. I didn't ask a lot of questions; I was just glad that she was out of our lives. Or so I thought.

But I really didn't have much time to think about her because our lives had become complicated. We, at Jack's mother's insistence, had moved in with Mrs. M, who was widowed, and had been diagnosed with dementia. Those were some tough, lonely years! At the time, I thought that Jack's late nights were because he found his mother's dementia too painful to face. Most days and evenings, up into the night, it was usually me, the sitter, and Mrs. M. Jack's brothers and their wives rarely made an appearance. Now I know where Jack was all those nights, and it wasn't at work.

Then one August, a few years after Mrs. M's death, Jack and I were vacationing at Amelia Island in Florida, when we received a frantic call from Gladys. Her son had been stabbed to death in a gang fight. I felt terrible for Gladys, but was a little confused as to why, after all these years, she would be calling Jack. Jack's reaction to the news was even more curious. He was fit to be tied to get back to town to check on Gladys. We were leaving the next morning anyway, so we made plans to leave extra early. I was still perplexed. When we got home, I fixed some ham and potato salad for Jack to take to Gladys. He dashed off to see her about midafternoon, but I didn't see him again until three or four the next morning. He was knee-walking drunk, I honestly don't see how he made it home in one piece. When I approached him about how long he had been gone, he said that nothing was going on, that they had lost track of time while they sat drinking and talking about her son. Outwardly, I accepted his explanation, but a little birdy was telling me that I was being a fool. The next morning, when I left for work, Jack was still sleeping. Passed out might be a more accurate term. When I got home around four o'clock in the afternoon, the telephone rang. I answered, and the voice on the other end identified himself as Gladys' "fiancé." He asked me, 'Do you know where your husband is?'

'I am assuming that he is at work,' was my reply.

Then he said, 'No, he's not. He is out here shacked up with my girlfriend, and has been all day. I want to know what you are going to do about it.'

Well, first I was going to try to breathe. Then I told him, 'Well, I can tell you what I am not going to do, I am not coming out to the projects!' I don't know who hung up first. Jack came home very late again, around four in the morning, very drunk. But this time, something had happened. Gladys' boyfriend had hit Jack over the head with a liquor bottle and thrown him out of the apartment into the bushes. A stick had gone into Jack's eye, and he was in agony, and drunk. Of course, I crawled out of bed and drove his sorry behind to the emergency room. The next day, the calls started, drunken calls, Gladys wanting to talk to Jack. After weeks of this, I told Jack it had better stop, that I had had enough. Surprisingly, the calls stopped, and I foolishly thought that Gladys was out of our lives forever! Silly me!

Until this day.

Fifteen years later.

Here I was with Fiona telling me that Gladys Cootye had never left our lives. Fiona told me that Gladys' sister constantly bragged to anyone who would listen about the affair. To prove it, Fiona told me some things about me and Jack and our families, that no one but us could have known. Personal things. Tidbits that could have come from only Jack. Then Fiona offered to show me where that piece of trash lived. Blindly, almost stumbling, I climbed into Fiona's Cadillac, and let her drive me by the low income apartment complex Gladys was now living in; Fiona pointed out which apartment was Gladys'. The apartments were about four blocks from my house, and two blocks from Jack's office in the opposite direction. Fiona then showed me the back alleys Jack used to go to Gladys' apartment during a workday. All through the entire tour, Fiona kept up a steady stream of stories and information, as well as providing a list of who knew about the affair. Then she asked me if I wanted to see where Gladys' worthless sister lived. I looked at Fiona, swallowed, and croaked, 'No, thank you, but I think I need to go home now, I think I might be sick.' She took me back to my car, and I, somehow, made it home. I was numb and hollow, I couldn't even cry.

When I pulled into the drive, I remembered that we were going to a movie. Going to a movie was the last thing I wanted to do right then. So was riding in a car with Jack. I somehow realized that I needed to be very careful with what I revealed to Jack. It was as if I were behind enemy lines. I dared not cry. I couldn't confront him and show my hand. I was sickened and frightened. I felt paralyzed, physically and emotionally. I didn't know how I was going to pull it off. I felt as if I were sleepwalking in a terrible nightmare. I opened the front door and called to Jack, telling him that I was home and just needed to walk the dogs before we left. When I was a ways from the house, I pulled out my cell phone and punched in Annie's number. I got her voicemail, so I left her a frantic message. I could hardly talk. I could barely breathe. In the message, I told Annie about The Pictures and about Gladys Cootye. I told Annie that I needed to get out of this farce of a marriage, but I didn't know how to do it, or if I could afford to do it. I told her that I was scared. Scared of staying, scared of leaving, and scared of being homeless. (Annie told me recently that she had saved that message so that, if I started to lose my nerve, she could play it back for me so that I could hear the fear, the hurt, and the heartbreak in my voice and in my words. She still has it. One day I'll listen to it).

I calmed myself, taking slow, steady breaths, and went back to the house with the dogs. The trip to the mall was long, quiet, and uneventful. We were still in our cool, civil mode from the aftermath of The Weekend. Thank goodness, I didn't have to talk to, or interact with Jack. I just quietly listened to the radio. We ended up going to see The Great Gatsby; I don't know how I managed to sit for two plus hours next to that man. My mind was slowly coming out of the stunned fog I had been in, and was racing overtime. Thoughts of all kinds were tumbling, jumbled, in my head. I absolutely could not concentrate on the movie, but it seemed loud and garish. To this day, I have not had the stomach to watch it again.

When we finally left the movie, Jack drove to Lens Crafters, and said that he was going in to get some lens cleaning materials. I told him that I would sit in the car and listen to the radio. Guess what? Unbelievable! Twice in two weeks! God had to be on my side! Jack had left his phone again! I don't know how I had the fortitude or presence of mind to act. But I did. I guess I'm tougher than I seem. I grabbed Jack's cell phone and scrolled through the telephone numbers he had dialed and calls he had received most recently, and jotted them down. When I got home, I looked up Gladys' number in the telephone book, and it, no surprise, was the number that was on his phone, over and over, day after day.

In the meantime, by the time Jack had returned to the car, I was calmly and quietly listening to the radio. We made it home and carried on with our usual routine. I don't know how, but I did. Inside, I felt like I was in someone else's very bad Lifetime movie. I walked and fed the dogs and the cats, fixed supper, and watched television. I felt small, I felt dead inside, I felt hopeless. Worst of all, I didn't feel cute any more.

Then I noticed that there was a voicemail message for me on my cell phone. I slipped away to the bathroom and listened to the message. It was Annie's strong, clear voice saying, 'Oh my God! We have got to get you away from that SOB. Charlie wants you to call his office Monday and come see him there. You have to do this!'

Chapter Six

And so, I began a life in subterfuge, living amidst lies and hidden secrets. Now I know how an undercover policeman or an undercover informant must feel. I had to keep acting as if nothing was going on and that life was perfectly normal, even though normal wasn't too great. In fact, my situation was a lot like the old saying about the duck on the pond: calm above the water, but paddling like hell underneath. I acted calm and the same as ever in our new frigid environment, but my brain was working like a washing machine on spin cycle. Thoughts of all kinds tumbled and fell about. All of the usual "shoulda, woulda, couldas," with the main theme being "How, how, how?" How could Jack do this to me? How could he have a mistress? How could he lie so easily and so much to me? How could I have taken this poor treatment for so long? How could I have been so blind, and not have known? How could he no longer think that I was cute?

Mama used to say that, if you aren't doing something like lying, stealing, or cheating yourself, then you are not going to suspect it, or look for it, in others. You know, something called honesty or trust. So, although the signs must have been there, I was trustingly oblivious. I wasn't looking for anything wrong, but his actions explain why he was always trying to accuse me of the things he was doing. Classic guilty conscience. In the "old days" when people would ask me how I could tolerate Jack's many misbehaviors, I always naively and proudly replied, "Well, he might drink too much and party to the extreme, but he always has an incredible sense of fairness, and he has never lied to me." Oh, good Lord! What a smug, insufferable, sad little sanctimonious fool I was! How could anyone take me seriously ever again? It makes me cringe now. I feel like I need to apologize to…everybody!

Then I started to get cold feet, and considered just putting everything behind me, and trying to get our lives back on track. I mean, at this point, I had talked to only a few discreet people, and I had not yet retained a lawyer. Then, I looked back on our lives and assessed what all had happened, and I knew that I could not get my life back on track because it had never been on track, at least not a good track. Also, I knew that if I gave up now, I would never have any kind of respect for myself again. And I would never expect anyone else to respect me either. Sometimes, easy is the wrong way to go, even if the right way promises to be very hard and absolutely terrifying. So, I pulled on my "big girl pants" and went to see my friend, Charlie, who, hopefully, would advise me, and steer me to a good divorce lawyer.

So, on Monday morning, I was perched in Charlie's office, feeling small and diminished, sad, and terribly, terribly embarrassed. And for some unknown reason, guilty. I guess I felt that if my life had come to this, I must have been doing something egregiously wrong in my marriage. I don't know why I was willing to even consider taking any of the blame. I was nervous and afraid that Charlie and my soon-to-be lawyer would judge me. I was going to have to learn how to shrug it off, and discard false and unearned guilt. Annie's husband, Charlie, handsome and brilliant, was a very successful lawyer, but he was not a divorce lawyer. He quickly realized that I needed a lawyer who was not from our county, and who would not be either intimidated by, or in cahoots with my in-laws. And I needed a good lawyer. Charlie was kind, and gently helped me see that I was following the only path and alternative that was left to me if I wanted to have any quality of life or a life at all. He made a telephone call to a lawyer who was a friend of his, as well as one of the best divorce lawyers in the state.

I could hear only one side of the conversation, but it was humiliating: "Yes, an alcoholic."

"Yes, abusive."

"Yes, yes, the usual, adultery."

Just hearing that made me realize what a mess this was. What had my life become? It was as tawdry and convoluted as my favorite soap operas, but sadly, not the least bit entertaining. At least, not to me. My appointment with my lawyer (oh my God! I had a lawyer!) was set up for the following week.

So, I had to go back home, and continue with our false life, but this time with an all-consuming secret. At least it was for just one more week, or so I thought. It was probably a good thing, at that time, that I foolishly didn't realize how long it would take to prepare for a divorce, and then to go through the whole divorce process. But I made it, one day at a time, all by myself.

The day of my appointment had arrived, and my sister and I traveled to the city, under the auspices of visiting some plant nurseries, a trip to Barnes and Noble, and lunch. I was clad in a blue and white striped seersucker shift and canvas espadrilles, carrying my Nantucket basket pocketbook, and of course, wearing my pearls. All of which probably screamed small-town Southern lady. I was feeling conflicted and nervous. And very, very guilty.

The law office was definitely uptown big city, and quite intimidating. Up we went to the fourth floor, glass and chrome with minimalist furnishings, quite tasteful. By the time my lawyer had made an appearance, I had calmed down some, partly because I had established a friendly connection with the receptionist whose husband had grown up in a small, rural community just outside of my hometown. What an incredibly small world we live in!

And then, Alan Kerr stepped from his office into the lobby, and I knew that Charlie had not steered me wrong. Alan was very tall, slim, well-dressed, with dark hair, blue eyes, and great dimples! He exuded an air of self-assurance and confidence. I felt an immediate affinity with him and felt that I could put my well-being in his hands with confidence. Maybe it was the dimples! I followed him into a quiet, beautiful conference room, it looked just like the ones in movies. There I met two paralegals who were professional, competent, and kind. They, especially the one named Emma, would become like lifelines to me. When we were seated, Alan and I discussed the business and monetary aspects, with most of it going in one ear and out the other. I was entirely too nervous and was concentrating on trying to calm the knot in my stomach and the lump in my throat. I nodded and agreed to everything even though I felt like I was completely in the dark. But I trusted Alan Kerr, and Charlie's intuition. Then it was my turn.

Right off the bat, I made it clear to Alan that I had been crazy about Jack Mallard since the moment I had laid eyes on him, and that I was still crazy about him, but that I could no longer live with him. And that it was breaking my heart. I told them that he had become someone and something that I no longer recognized. Then I recounted some of the abuse, told them about The Pictures and the mistress, described Jack's rampant alcoholism, and explained the fact that we lived in Jack's parents' house, which Jack owned with his brothers. I explained the situation: that I had nowhere to go and nowhere to live, that I had no family to take me in. I also told him that I did not want that money-pit of a mausoleum, I just needed somewhere to live until other arrangements could be made. I also told him about The Tapes. Throughout this interminable meeting, I somehow managed to control my tears, although I desperately wanted to weep and wail. However, I also wanted to act like a dignified adult, and not the scared little crybaby that I felt like. At the end of the consultation and meeting, we had a plan. Alan, on his end, would immediately start the work on the separation papers, an order from a judge for me to remain, temporarily, in the house, and to contact and line up a private investigator. I, on my end, was to gather up everything that was pertinent, list all my assets, and bring all of this, with a financial statement, to our next appointment.

Drained, I numbly thanked him, and rose to leave. Alan stood, smiled kindly at me, and as he shook my hand, said, 'Your husband is a fool. You are the real deal – you are beautiful and intelligent, and you are charming.' I thanked him again and left before I could break down in tears. I figured that Alan probably told every shattered woman who sat in that chair the same thing. But it helped. And it worked. I walked out of his office, chin in the air, ready to do battle.

*****

I returned home, and discreetly gathered what the lawyer would need when the time came, and prepared my financial statement, which didn't take very long. But it seemed that everything else was moving slowly at a snail's pace. Also, I was very concerned about the fact that Alan had not retained and fired up the private investigator yet. For some pathetic paranoid reason, I was terrified that the investigator might not be able to catch Jack with his mistress if he didn't hurry up. I don't know why I was afraid that Jack would suddenly deviate from his routine after more than twenty years. Just jitters, I guess.

As I waited, inwardly impatient, but outwardly calm, cool, and collected, life at home continued in our new norm. We still practiced the cool, distant attitude and politely civil tone. Obviously, we were both good fakers. Not that there weren't any new incidents. There always were. What is sad is that, after these incidents, Jack never apologized or seemed to feel bad about what was said or done. What is even sadder, and verged on sick, is the fact that I never forced the issue. I was scared that it would ignite another incident, or even worse and sadder, that he might leave. Most nights, Jack, with his alarmingly increasing drunkenness, usually passed out in his chair downstairs, and I no longer made any attempts to coax him awake to go upstairs to bed. There were still those nights that, in spite of my prayers, he would make his way upstairs. Cruel, hateful, bitter, just plain mean. And my little friend on the bedside table diligently recorded it all.

Most of my communication with the law office and Alan was through Emma, one of Alan's extremely competent and kind paralegals. She usually contacted me on my cell phone during the day, when I was at work. At the time, I was working in a cute gift and garden shop, and usually had plenty of free time and privacy. Finally, the call I had been anxiously awaiting came. Emma called and gave me the name and telephone number of the private investigator that Alan's firm used. Emma told me that the investigator was very good and very discreet. Then she reminded me that getting the goods on Jack and that woman might take a while, but to just stay calm. She said that once the investigator had gotten the evidence that we needed, we would finally be ready to make a move. Alan wanted all the proverbial "ducks in a row" before we served any papers on Jack and got the ball rolling. I felt relieved, frightened, charged up, and strangely sad.

I made the call to the private investigator, and he was very pleasant, very professional, and very reassuring. We discussed the mistress, and when I thought Jack usually visited her. Then I gave him the mistress' address, telephone number, the kind of car she drove, and then, a description of Jack, his office address, and a description of his car. Mr.

Vance, the investigator, said that he would come to my shop the next day so that I could sign the contract and provide him with a photograph of Jack. After we hung up, I felt weak and jittery, and consumed with guilt, sadness, and regret. It was really happening, and now that it was, I didn't know if I was ready.

When I got home that day, Jack was not there. So what's new. He also was not at his office. I knew, not because I was stalking him, but because I had to drive by his office on my way home from work. I did the usual routine, I walked the dogs, fed the dogs and cats, straightened up the house, and fixed supper. A very nice supper, by the way. I had long ago given up waiting to eat evening meals with Jack. He either came home late, late, late (and drunk), or if he came home at a reasonable time, he would usually sit on the porch and listen to a sports radio show that he liked, while consuming vast quantities of Scotch. He would eat, if he ate, after ten o'clock at night, which was too late for me.

That night, after I had fixed supper, and had it warming on the stove, I plopped down to watch something on the television. Jack finally came home, very late, very drunk, and very irritable. To avoid any unpleasantness, I left his supper on the stove, and went upstairs to read a book. I heard him come into the house from the porch, talking on his cell phone. A few minutes later, he shouted up the stairs, angrily saying something about not wanting to eat what I had cooked. Then everything was eerily quiet for a while. I lay there praying that he had passed out. No such luck. My heart jerked, because I could hear him coming slowly up the stairs, muttering, and stumbling. When he came to a stop at the foot of the bed, I steeled myself, looked up from my book, smiled, and invited him to get in the bed and watch whatever he wanted on the television.

He moved closer and leaned over the bed until his face was about six inches from mine, and said, in a sneering, contemptuous snarl, 'I refuse to spend the night! With you! In this house!'

I blinked in surprise, and tried to reason with him (I knew better, you can never reason with a drunk), and said, 'Oh, don't be silly! If you really want to sleep alone, there are four other bedrooms and all the beds are made.'

He shouted, in reply, 'I don't want to stay here with you! YOU. STUPID. F*****G C**T!' I felt the air leave my body. I did not know what in the world was going on, but I was frightened.

A terrifying thought came to me and fear stabbed at my heart. All I could think was, 'Oh, my God, maybe he's leaving me before I can leave him!'

Then he said, 'I'm going to spend the night at my office. But I am going to walk, because I don't want to get a DUI.'

A light bulb lit up in my brain – a 100-watt floodlight bulb. I knew where he was going. I knew that there were no comfortable chairs in his office and nowhere to sleep comfortably. I might be slow, but I'm not stupid. He was going to his mistress' apartment. He turned and staggered out of the room, and lumbered down the stairs. I leaped into action! Oh. My. GOD! It was happening!

I grabbed my cardigan sweater and pulled it on over my nightgown, and ran to the head of the stairs. I could hear him in the den, on the phone again. Then he staggered down the hall, and slammed out the front door. I flew down the stairs and watched out the front door to see where he was headed. He walked down the drive, and turned right onto the sidewalk outside the front gate. I grabbed my car keys and ran out the door, flew down the front steps, and raced to my car. I cranked the car, backed it up, turned around, and, without turning on the lights, let the car coast down the drive until I was at the front gate.

I peeked to the right to see where Jack was. He was standing at the end of our street at the stop sign, and then he turned left. I crept the car out onto the street and up to the stop sign and looked left, down the street. Jack was standing at the end of the street, on the comer. Then he turned right, and shambled along the sidewalk of the main road. Oh, boy! He was traveling the long way, probably because it was well-lit. Well, I knew the back way, the shortcut! There is nothing like being in your own hometown, your briar patch! I gunned the car across the main road when the light changed, and made my way by back streets to the street that the mistress' low income apartment complex occupied. I pulled into the bushes, across the street from the apartments, as far into the bushes as I could, and then cut the car and the lights off, and waited. About ten minutes later, Jack appeared out of the dark, walking along the sidewalk. He stopped right behind my car. I stopped breathing, praying that he wouldn't see my car, or me sitting in my car, deep in the bushes. Thank the Lord, it was dark, and he was drunk, and completely oblivious to his surroundings. He lit a cigarette, and then crossed the street to her ground-floor apartment. He rapped on the apartment window with a secret knock he used to use at his brother Mark's house, and then entered her apartment. I think that I might have been on the verge of hyperventilating. My heart was pounding so hard that it made my chest hurt, and I could hear it pounding in my ears. I could not breathe. My hands were shaking so badly that I couldn't hold my phone. I had tried to take a picture of Jack entering the apartment, but my phone was wobbling and shaking so much that I was scared I might drop the phone out of the car window. I was in a full-fledged panic. Thank goodness, no one's life depended on me that night, I was in pitiful shape.

Desperately, I tried to think of whom I could call this late at night. Finally, I decided to try to call the private investigator. All of a sudden, I couldn't remember if I had grabbed my pocketbook when I grabbed my keys. But there it was! I reached in and snatched up my address book. I made myself take slow, deep breaths, trying to steady my nerves and calm myself enough so that I could punch in the investigator's number. Finally! I was steadying, it had probably been only a few minutes, but it felt like an eternity. Finally! I did it! The investigator's phone was ringing!

I kept whispering, 'Please answer. Please answer.'

He did. I could hardly talk. I finally got the words out. Patiently, he calmed me down. I told him that Jack was in his mistress' apartment, and that I thought that he was going to spend the night. Mr. Vance asked me what Jack was wearing.

I told him, 'He's very handsome, and has short, light-brown hair. He wears wire rims. He is wearing a white, short-sleeved, button-down shirt with khaki pants. And he's wearing his loafers. He looks very nice!' Pathetic!

Mr. Vance verified the address and the apartment number, and said, 'Okay, Mrs. M., you go home now, and get some rest. We've got it from here.'

In a panic, I cried, 'I haven't signed the papers yet!'

He replied, 'It's alright, we'll do that tomorrow when we meet. Where would you like to meet us?' We decided on the Walmart parking lot. Then he said, 'Go home, we'll be in touch.'

*****

So, home I went. But there was absolutely no possibility of getting any rest. I was beside myself, and positively manic. I was jittery, I couldn't sit still, my mind was going like a whirling dervish. I needed something to do! I rushed about the house, gathering up all the guns and bullets, and put them in duffle bags, which I then put in my car, and locked it. While I was buzzing around feverishly in the downstairs, I saw that Jack had, once again, left his phone. God is good! I picked it up and pressed a button, and looked at the last number that he had called. It was Gladys' number. I decided that I should take a picture of the number, since it was the mistress' number with the date and the time. I found my camera and took a closeup. Then…well, then I shouted out loud, 'Oh, Hell with it!' Then grabbed the phone and ran to put it in the glove box of my car. I carefully locked the car. Then I kept trying to lie down and get some rest, but I could not stay still. I roamed about the house, intermittently watching television, then trying to read a book, and then walking the poor dogs, again and again.

I think I willed the sun to finally come up. Still no sign of Jack, and no word from the investigator. Thank goodness, my sister is an early riser. I called her when I thought she might be up, and took the artillery and the cell phone to her house for safekeeping. Still no word from the investigator. Earlier in the week, I had made plans with my neighbor to go blueberry picking. To keep up appearances of normality, I decided to carry on, and do everything I normally would. So, my neighbor and I left around 8:30 in the morning. It was a gloriously beautiful day, and picking the berries and casually chatting with my friend calmed me, and actually brought a sense of determination and strength to me. However, I did not mention or even hint at my woes to my neighbor. I was afraid that I might blow everything if I told anyone. Still no message from my investigator. I could not eat. I could not rest. I could not turn my brain off.

Finally. Twelve-thirty p.m., a call from Mr. Vance! We were to meet in front of the garden section of Walmart. Mr. Vance told me that he and his partner would be in a black Tahoe. I pulled into the parking lot, and immediately spotted them. With my heart in my throat, I climbed out of my car, and approached the driver's side of the Tahoe.

I smiled, and asked, 'Mr. Vance?'

'Yes,' was the reply.

Before he could say anything more, his partner jumped in and exclaimed, 'Ma'am? My God! I just want to say that our mouths literally dropped open when you stepped out of your car! You are very attractive, and charming! Not what we expected! Usually, it's the opposite. You know. The wife looks like crap, and the girlfriend looks great, but...'

Mr. Vance then interrupted with, 'Mrs. M, have. Have you seen this woman?'

I hesitated, and then said, 'I haven't seen her in close to twenty years, but all I can say is that back then, she was pretty rough, and I hate to say it, but an awfully tacky redneck.'

Mr. Vance nodded, and added, 'Well, that about describes her! She looked so bad and so old, we thought she was your husband's girlfriend's mother!'

Wow! How mortifying! Then he had me look at enough of the video to ensure that they had caught the right philanderer and woman on film. They had. Jack had been in her apartment for over fourteen hours. The investigators told me that they followed him when he left Gladys' apartment, and that he had walked to his office. Then Mr. Vance told me that he would send the video to my lawyer for him to see if it would be enough. Mr. Vance thought that it would be all that was needed. I signed the contract, and thanked him for rallying and coming to my rescue. Although I didn't hear from Alan's office for several days, it turned out that the video was more than enough. I had hired a private investigator for just one day!

When Jack came home later that day, it was midafternoon. I had somehow calmed down; it was probably just exhaustion and running out of adrenaline. I felt like the walking dead. I acted normal and pleasant, but very cool. Jack kept looking in drawers, under cushions, and under chairs. Finally, I innocently asked him, in an interested, concerned voice, what he was looking for, and could I help? He said that he had misplaced his phone. How I kept a straight face, I do not know. I acted perplexed, and suggested that maybe he had dropped it the night before when he had walked to his office. Asking which route he had taken to his office, I offered to walk the route with him to help look for his phone. He declined – thank goodness. I shrugged, and went on with my everyday activities of a normal day and life. I had already decided that, as soon as I got the word from Alan that the video was a go, I was going to move back into the guestroom, permanently. But oh my, I had such mixed feelings. I wanted to get away from Jack, but yet, I didn't want to let go. I wanted a new, tranquil life, but I was terrified to let go of the old. In fact, I was petrified. The only bright spot that I could see was that I would not have to pretend or hide for much longer.

Chapter Seven

About a week later, I went to Alan's office to read through all of the papers, and make any corrections that were needed. Emma said that they would re-do the papers with all of the corrections, and then, at that point, everything would be a go. Then we would be able to get things really rolling shortly thereafter. I had the tape recorder with me, and asked Emma if they wanted it. She said not right then, maybe later. I was a little perplexed at their lack of interest in my recordings; I don't think that they realized just what was on those tapes. They must have thought that the tapes were some petty he-said, she-said, fussing and complaining. Boy, were they in for a surprise!

Actually, I was a little relieved that I was able to keep the tapes a little longer. They helped me with my resolve. Whenever I began to feel myself weakening or doubting myself, or considering not going through with the divorce, all I had to do was hit the play button on the recorder and listen. As soon as I heard Jack's sneering, contemptuous, drunken voice, my stomach would feel queasy, and would knot up, and my heart would cringe. It didn't even matter what was being said, just the tone of his voice, the cruel contempt, was all it took to strengthen my resolve, and make me reaffirm that I was doing the only thing I could if I wanted to remain sane and alive.

Then the week before the Fourth of July, I got the call. The papers were to be served the next week. I'm sorry, think what you want of me, but I called Alan's office and begged Emma for them to put off serving the papers for one more week. I didn't want to ruin everyone's Fourth of July plans. Yes, I know, I am a fool, but at least I am a nice fool!

During the past couple of weeks, I had been trying to let some of Jack's family know that something was amiss. I guess I was trying to give Jack and his family one more chance to do something to help that would change my mind. For some reason, Bob and Trudy, who lived several hours away, had been coming to town and visiting quite frequently. They had their own house here that they used for holidays and family weekends. For weeks, I had been hinting to Trudy that things had become pretty bad between me and Jack, in the hopes that she and Bob might step in and help us.

Nothing.

I gutted it up and told Trudy about how Jack talked to me, and that he had started grabbing me by the neck and threatening me.

Nothing.

I even confided in her about The Pictures. Nothing.

Finally, the last weekend that we were together, I told her that I did not know how much longer I could stand my situation, or even stay in the marriage.

Still nothing.

That same last weekend, the four of us were "Sunday driving" around town, and we passed by Gladys Cootye's old project (not her current residence). Someone made a remark about the project. I thought, *here's my chance to let Jack come clean, and then maybe we can start over.* I know, pathetic. Trudy and I were in the backseat, so I leaned forward, and said, 'Jack used to have a secretary who lived here. Gladys Cootye. Jack, whatever happened to her?'

All he had to say was something like, 'You know what? She is in a bad way. In fact, I go by her apartment sometimes, and try to help her out.'

Nothing.

Instead, he said, 'I don't know.'

Ohhh. What a liar! So, now, our fate was sealed. If only he had told me the truth or even a partial truth. He had to know that I suspected something if I brought her name up after all these years. Well, sometimes you have to know when to give up, and move on. So, I was going to leave behind over thirty years of repression and hurt, and try to find myself again.

*****

The Day had arrived, and I was scared and so very, very heartsick and heart weary. Emma had called the day before, and had told me that the papers would be served on Jack sometime today. She felt that I needed to not be there when it happened. Jack would have to leave the house, and I could then return safely. There would be a restraining order in place, because I was afraid that he might, in a drunken rage, come back and try to kill me. I got up early that morning, as usual, let the dogs out, and went into the kitchen to make coffee. Jack was passed out downstairs in his chair. I stood for a while, just looking at him, knowing that it was probably for the last time, and trying to memorize every line and contour of his handsome face. He still looked beautiful to me. For a while, a brief while, he seemed at peace. He was seldom at peace, there were usually too many demons fighting inside of him.

I fed the animals, and then took the dogs to the groomer, and asked him if I could leave the dogs with him until five o'clock. He said that they would be fine with him. Then I went home, and to tell the truth, I was so upset, I'm not sure what I did to pass the time. More than likely, I made the bed and cleaned the house while I waited for Jack to get dressed, so that I could tell him that I was leaving him. Everyone had told me to just leave for the day, that he didn't deserve any kind of consideration. But I wanted him to know ahead of time, because I didn't want him to be blindsided and look foolish in front of the processors. First, he needed to get dressed! I didn't want him to be in his robe when he was served, I wanted him to have some dignity. But he piddled around all morning, as usual. He went into the bathroom and read the paper for what seemed like hours! I kept praying that he would hurry up and get dressed.

Eleven o'clock, the phone rang. It was Annie, 'Where are you? I thought you were coming here. Get out of that house!'

I told her that I'd be there in a few minutes, but that I had to talk to Jack. She said that if I wasn't at her house soon, she was going to come and get me. I hung up the phone, walked to the bathroom door, and gently knocked.

I heard Jack sigh, and then an irritated, 'Yes?'

'Jack, I have to talk to you. It's important.'

He replied angrily, saying, 'Can't it wait?'

I took a deep, shaky breath, cracked the door, and said, 'Jack, I know about Glenda, and I know about Gladys Cootye. Decent people don't live like this. I am leaving you. You will be served with papers today. So, please, you had better get dressed.'

I turned and fled the house. As I slammed the front door, I heard him behind me in the hall, telling me to stop. But I had to go then! Or I might not be able to go at all. I didn't know how I was going to make it without Jack in my life. I had been with him for over thirty years, through "the good, the bad, and the ugly." I made it to the car and drove to Annie's.

I spent the entire day at Annie's. She and her two darling children did their best to keep me entertained. The children didn't understand what was going on, but they could tell that I was upset, and they, along with Annie, did their best to keep my mind off of what was happening, or not happening. We kept getting reports from Alan's office that the processors had experienced some kind of holdup. So, I spent the entire day, hollow, diminished, and scared, wondering when this day would ever end. At five o'clock, I had to go get my dogs. (Thankfully, I had thought to leave extra dry food for my cats that morning.) I went, with my dogs, to my sister's house, as I did not think that I should impose myself, now with dogs, any longer on Annie.

Finally, after dark, I got the call from the processor that the papers had been served. The processor paused, and then told me that he and his partner, I guess everyone travels in pairs, had read the papers before they served them, and that they were horrified, disgusted, and outraged. He said that no one should ever be allowed to treat another person the way Jack had obviously treated me. Then the processor gave me their number, saying that if I ever felt like I was in danger from Jack or his family to call them.

Since it was so late, the dogs and I spent the night at my sister's. She lived in a cute little bungalow that, unfortunately, had only one bedroom. So, I lay, sleepless, on the sofa until morning. When the sun came up, the dogs and I returned home. Thank goodness, no one was there. I was relieved, I wanted to be alone. I felt sad and empty, as did the house. Suddenly, the land line and my cell phone both began to ring loudly and simultaneously. And so, it had begun.

*****

Oh, yes, the nasty mess of the divorce had begun. My phones were ringing off the hook, texts were binging, and friends were ringing the doorbell. They not only came by my house, but they also came by work, and stopped me on the street. Most of them were very concerned for me, all were curious. It's funny what you learn about people and friends when times get messy or tough. Jack had an old college friend who used to be in politics. He had his own plane, and after he returned from a trip to South America, he was arrested by federal agents, upon landing, for smuggling marijuana. He was convicted and did hard time in a federal penitentiary. One of his favorite sayings was, "There's nothing like going to jail to separate the wheat from the chaff among your friends." Very true, but I'd like to add, "There's nothing like divorce to separate the wheat from the chaff among your friends." It will completely surprise you who is wheat, and who is chaff.

Most of my friends were concerned and supportive of my decision. Some friends were on the fence and stayed there, neither supportive nor accusatory, and I respected their stand. Some friends completely turned their backs on me, and avoided me like the plague – definitely chaff. Then there was the rotten chaff, "friends" who, in the past, had courted me to get in with my in-laws, and then had pretty much dropped me once their goal had been accomplished. After my separation, these repugnant friends began to come around again, acting very concerned, trying to pick my brain. Oh, well, like they say, "With friends like that, who needs enemies." It's funny, not only do some people think that kindness is a sign of weakness, but they also must think that kindness is a sign of stupidity. It's not!

Then there were the people who came out of the woodwork with information. These people had always kept quiet because they did not know what to do or say, or who to approach. Some thought that I had known about the mistress, and had chosen to ignore it. It didn't matter to me, I was not angry or hurt, I understood the uncomfortable or awkward position in which they had found themselves. I was absolutely blown away by the flood of information that flowed my way. It helped to strengthen me in my decision to end my marriage.

Innumerable friends, with a sense of relief at unloading their burden, told me that Jack, in his drunken ramblings, had often referred to a girlfriend. But Gladys Cootye's sister inadvertently provided the most damaging evidence. She seemed to be inordinately proud of the fact that her sister was having a sordid affair with a Mallard. How pathetic is that, and what does it say about their upbringing? She bragged about it to anyone who would listen. Although we didn't run in the same social circles, she came in contact with three of my friends. One was, of course, Fiona, who, thank goodness, spilled it all after sitting on the information for years. Another friend had immediately dismissed it as positively ludicrous, and as a result, had not listened to the prideful ramblings. The third friend didn't know what to do with the information, so she sat on it until the time for clarity had arrived. The sister's proud prattlings provided Jack's coffin and the nails. Her endless chatter revealed that Jack had often complained about me, and had told Gladys and her sister intimate information about our relationship and our marriage. The worst was that Jack had told them that he had married the wrong girl.

Also, this terrible woman bragged that Jack ate lunch almost every day with Gladys, and most evenings he ate supper with them. As heartbreaking as all of this was, it was incredibly illuminating, and helped explain a lot about my relationship with Jack. But the worst part of all wasn't so much the reality of the mistress, it was the betrayal, that he had talked badly about me and complained about me behind my back to that woman and her nasty sister.

Some of my friends felt so badly about what they perceived as letting me down that they actually wept. I assured them, and all of the friends who came forward, that their timing had been perfect, that I would not have had all the necessary ammunition, like The Tapes, before now. But there was so much more. Another friend, who worked in a restaurant/bar, told me that Jack had come to the restaurant on several occasions and ordered two take-out dinners (with she-crab soup, no less), and then would warn her that he had never been there. Our old friend Madison finally admitted that, on several occasions, Jack had brought Gladys to his house for the weekend so that they could stay together and party. He also said that, whenever he came to visit in our town that Jack would take him over to the mistress' apartment to grill steaks and party. Madison was very sheepish about his confessions.

Then some of the women who lived in Gladys Cootye's apartment complex gleefully filled me in with all kinds of tidbits. They shopped at the IGA, as did I, and when they realized who I was, they could not wait to talk to me. None of them cared for Gladys at all, they thought that she was rude, crude, nasty, and foul-mouthed. According to them, Jack visited Gladys every day. Apparently, he brazenly pulled his car up to the front entrance of the apartment building, would get his liquor and her beer out of the car, and then walk openly down the hall to Gladys' apartment. These ladies had nicknamed Jack, The Beer Man. Usually, Gladys would be out in the hall, waiting, loudly telling everyone that Jack was her man, her boyfriend. The ladies also told me that Gladys had an extensive porn collection, and was a loud, nasty drunk, as well as a drug addict, often trading sex with a local drug dealer for drugs. Yes, Jack must have married the wrong girl if this was what tickled his fancy.

Also, some of the men who used to work for Jack called me, and almost tearfully apologized for not telling me what had been going on, but they had been afraid of losing their jobs. I thanked them for coming forward and assured them that there was no way that I blamed them for anything. One of the men who had worked the longest with Jack told me that Jack and that woman started their relationship almost as soon as Gladys started working for Jack, which was before Jack and I were married. He said that Gladys would brag every day at work to all who would listen about what she and Jack had done, when they did it, how many times, and would provide details of exactly how. He told me that he and the rest of the men were disgusted and sickened, and that none of them could understand what was going on in Jack's head. The first thing Jack did when he was served with papers was to drive to this man's house and threaten him to say nothing.

Some people tried to console me with the "all men do it" mantra. I calmly explained that I probably would have forgiven some brief, midlife crisis fling with some cute, young thing, but not this. This twenty plus year affair with an old alcoholic, drug-addled, nasty piece of trash. Then one friend consoled me with, 'At least it wasn't a wealthy, beautiful, sophisticated woman.'

I stared at her in disbelief, and said, 'That, I would have understood! This, I don't and never will!'

So, even though all of this was devastating, and diminishing, and mortifyingly embarrassing to me, it was also enlightening and helped me tremendously by hardening and toughening me and my resolve. I salute and thank all my friends for their courage and help, and for shedding light on the whole distasteful and hurtful situation. Yes, knowledge is power, but knowledge is also empowerment.

*****

It was quite moving for me that people all around town tried to help me in many different ways. I sometimes proofread at a small, local newspaper. The staff was all-female, so it was a comfortable environment. I think that the girls thought that I might be missing having a man in my life, since I was going through a very long divorce, and living alone. So, one day, one of the girls handed me a bag with some paperback books in it. She had a secretive, knowing look on her face, and said, 'Miss M*****, we thought you might like to read these at bedtime.' I took the package. When I got home, I looked in the bag. It was the series of "Fifty Shades" books.

I thought, *Oh, what the hell! Why not, I'll give them a try.* I read the first couple of chapters, then started skimming, and then just gave up and closed the book for good. I found the premise and the book a little disturbing. And maybe a little too familiar.

So, I packed the books up, and returned them the next day. When I handed Tammy the books, she winked at the other girls, and said, with a sly smile, 'Too racy for you, Miss M****?'

'No,' I said, with a smile, 'Been there. Done it all. Didn't particularly like it then. Don't want to read about it.' I smiled at them, thanked them for thinking of me, and bid them a great day. Then I winked, and left them all with their mouths open.

Chapter Eight

We are now delving into the meat of the separation and divorce proceedings. I had immediately become a persona non grata with all of my in-laws. In today's slang, they were attempting to ice me out, but it was worse than that. Myrna Rae would literally and physically turn her back on me whenever she saw me. On the street, in a store, in a restaurant, at a party. Or at a community function. She made sure that I was dropped from many social activities, such as a lunch crowd or a club. I didn't fret too much about that because most of those things weren't my cup of tea anyway. It would have been laughable if it weren't so real and so intentionally hurtful. Needless to say, initially, I was very taken aback and hurt by the angry, coldly furious attitude and cruel dismissal of me by all of that family. But I refused to stoop to their level, and was always cordial and polite to them, the old adage of kill them with kindness.

So, I always quietly smiled and politely spoke even when it was to a turned back. They were the ones who looked bad, from the front or the back. It seemed that I looked at a lot of backs and backsides back then.

After the separation, Jack made just one halfhearted attempt to talk to me, after that he was barely civil; actually, he was rude, angry, and threatening. If he saw me somewhere, I could feel and see nothing but barely suppressed hate and cold fury. Typical of his family, he never, ever felt like he had done anything wrong. None of them have ever been held accountable for how they mistreat people. I think that it shocked them all that this sensitive, tender-hearted, people-pleaser adjusted her attitude and came out swinging.

During all of this upheaval, I tried very hard to suppress the big crybaby that was inside of me. I tried to save most of my feeling sorry for myself for when I was at home, at night, or in the car when I was driving alone. I didn't want people to feel awkward around me. But believe me, big girls do cry. For months, I cried every day and every night with great, ragged sobs that sounded like they were originating from deep in my gut. Then, one day, the tears stopped. Maybe I was just cried out, or maybe I had finally decided that it was time to grow up, toughen up, pull on my big girl pants, and face down the clan. It was difficult at first; I had been an integral part of the family for over thirty years, and suddenly, here I was, out, exposed. Completely on my own. One thing that I had finally figured out was that everyone was so angry with me because Jack had always been my problem to handle, and now, he wasn't my problem anymore, he had become their problem. Nevertheless, my problems with these people were just beginning to come to a head. Their bullying and intimidation tactics just served to bring out the notoriously stubborn, hardheadedness in me. The gloves were off. Bring it on!

*****

96

The day of our first day in court before a judge had finally arrived; it had been almost three months since the separation had begun. The main reason for the lengthy delay was that we had to wait for a judge from another county to cycle through for our hearing. The family court judge from our county had had to recuse himself because he knew all of us personally. Alan and I were already in the courtroom settling in when the clan arrived. I was shocked to see not only Jack with his lawyer, but also Jack's brothers with their lawyers in tow. All of them, lawyers and Mallards, were pushing carts loaded with stacks of boxes laden with folders and papers.

I leaned towards Alan, and whispered, worriedly, 'What in the world is in all of those boxes and folders? I haven't done enough, good or bad, in my whole life to fill even one folder.'

Alan dimpled at me, and said, 'They probably have old phone books and obsolete files in those boxes. They are just trying to rattle you.' Then, he added, 'You know, you really lucked out, this judge hates bullies. Now, what do you think that looks like over there?' He nodded towards the legal convention that had assembled at the other table.

I calmed down some almost immediately. He was right, of course. I looked over at Jack's table again with seven men sitting there with their towers of files behind them, and compared it to my table with just me and my one lawyer with his one briefcase. Remember, both brothers-in-law were probably banking on the fact that not only were both of them lawyers in their own right, albeit mediocre, but they were also both in politics. No doubt about it. Definitely bullies.

Alan had instructed me that only lawyers would be talking today, that I was to just sit quietly and jot down anything important that came to mind. Thank goodness! I was so nervous that my mouth was dry and my hands were shaking. My heart was in my throat, and pounding. Alan and a lawyer from the clan table handed the judge copies of our financial statements, and the hearing began.

The main objective of this hearing was to ensure that I could remain, temporarily, in the home, and to try to get some type of financial help or allowance for me. Jack's main lawyer stood and addressed the judge, and agreed that I could remain in the house until the divorce was final. (Don't worry about Jack, he was living in his brother's holiday house, for free.) Then the lawyer told the judge, 'As to an allowance, Mr. Mallard makes only about twelve hundred dollars a month, and cannot afford to give his wife any money. He feels that she is educated and employable.' (Of course, that was bogus, the electric bill alone at our house was close to twelve hundred dollars a month!)

The judge leaned forward over his desk, and said, 'Now, let me get this straight. This is your strategy: sure, we'll put a roof over her head, and then, we'll starve her out.'

Then he sat back, and picked up a sheath of papers and began going through them. He glanced at Jack and his legal group, cleared his throat, and said, 'Mr. Mallard, I am sitting here, looking at your financial statement. It looks like you, with your family, own over a hundred fifty different tracts of land, two subdivisions, a shopping center, a beach house, and several other lots on the beach. You also have river property, an historical home, a mountain house, and quite a few rental properties. You receive dividends from five banks and a large investment portfolio. Why, it looks to me like you are worth at least several million dollars! I think that you can afford to help your wife out. Don't you?'

Oh, my! Hope does spring eternal, and prayers are sometimes answered. Victory feels fantastic! I was practically walking on air as we left the courtroom. We were able to slip right out while Jack and his private bar association entourage fumbled around, looking stunned, and packing up their carts. Alan and I walked together to where our cars were parked. I was thanking him effusively. He smiled at me, and said, 'Let's meet at my office next week. Now that things are finally moving along, we can begin to work on some strategy. I'll have Emma call you this afternoon to set things up.' We said goodbye and separated to go to our cars.

Alan stopped and looked back at me, 'Oh, and bring those tapes you keep talking about.'

I grinned. Well, hallelujah! At last!

*****

Next week arrived before I could take a deep breath. So, back to the big city, to the law office building, up to the fourth floor, and into the august, imposing conference room. I was seated at a long table with Alan, a female associate, and three female paralegals – lots of girl power. We had a round table discussion about strategies, hearings, mediation, depositions, and discovery. None of which I could seem to completely grasp; I think my poor brain was on overload. These people, all of them, were so smart and so organized. I felt more and more confident because of their competence. For the first time, I truly felt that I was probably going to be alright.

It was decided that there was really no way to move forward too much until they could receive Jack's telephone and email records, detailed descriptions of his assets, as well as his credit card and bank records. It was decided that the discovery request would be sent to Jack's main lawyer, although we were all a little confused about which lawyer out of the Mallard legal convention was the one truly in charge. Alan decided that we should give Jack three months to gather and provide all of his discovery, which meant that it would be due in January. Thus, we were going to be, more or less, at a standstill until then. How frustrating! The creaky, slow wheels of justice! I had no idea that a divorce, a childless divorce, would drag along like this.

Then Alan looked over at me, and said, 'Well, let's have a listen at those tapes!'

I handed him the recorder, explaining that the really revealing, frighteningly disturbing recordings were in the middle and at the end. Alan, disregarding me, hit the button at the beginning, which was, to me, the relatively mild stuff. As soon as I heard Jack's voice, that drunken, sneering tone, my heart took the old familiar dive and my stomach knotted up, I was staring down at my lap, feeling so ashamed – and this was mild! Then I heard it: gasps, intake of breath, whispers of "Oh, my God." I looked up. I had assumed that, since this was one of the most prestigious divorce firms in the state, they had heard it all before, and that they would be inured to this type of verbal abuse, that it would be old hat to them. I looked around. All four women were gasping with their hands over their mouths.

Alan looked stunned, and ill. He muttered, 'I can't listen to another word of this!' Then he leaned forward and hit the stop button. He turned to me, and asked, 'You married that bum?'

I felt everyone's eyes on me. I didn't know what to say. I was so mortifyingly embarrassed. I nodded, and said, 'But he used to not be that bad. Not when we first started dating.' I stopped. Nothing but pitying looks were coming my way. I gave up trying to protect Jack, and said, 'You're right, he's really awful. Wait until you hear the really bad stuff.'

Their expressions said that they couldn't believe that there could be anything any worse on the tapes. I wanted to say, "Just wait!"

Alan and everybody in the conference room agreed that, because of background noise, we needed to get the tapes cleaned up and transcribed onto paper. It was decided to get an expert company that transcribed tapes professionally to do the work. Of course, it would take some time. However, we had at least three months since we were waiting for Jack's discovery. I knew, even though I didn't say a word, that Jack would never have his discovery ready in three months. He was the ultimate procrastinator. This was going to be a very long divorce, an exercise in unending embarrassment and shame, a nightmare without end. But the group's gasping, gut-wrenching reaction to the tapes made me realize, at last, that I wasn't being a silly, whiney, crybaby. My fears were real. I finally realized that I was slowly climbing upward out of a pit of hopelessness into the light of hope.

Well, the three months actually went by rather quickly, mainly because it was the holiday season. The law office kept in touch throughout those months with plenty of telephone calls and all kinds of paperwork in the mail. Finally, January came to an end. Guess what? Big surprise. No discovery.

February. No discovery. March. No discovery.

I don't know if the Mallard clan couldn't handle Jack, or if this was some kind of perverted strategy, that maybe, if they dragged everything out long enough, that I would give up and go back to Jack. Right. So, he could turn around and divorce me. He didn't want me back. Even I could see that, hurtful as it was.

As spring approached with still no discovery, Alan decided that we should do something to move the process along. So, he decided to go ahead with some depositions. The law office drew up the papers to be served on the two girlfriends. I warned Alan and Emma that they would probably play hell getting Glenda served, as she was a vagrant and slept anywhere she could; she often traded sex for a place to sleep. Those poor processors! They were never able to serve papers on Glenda. I kept calling the processors with sightings. A couple of times, she was actually strolling down the sidewalk in front of my house. Alan finally gave up on her, especially after he got copies of her criminal records. She was in jail every few weeks for vagrancy, shoplifting, and/or public drunk. Alan decided that Glenda would be too unreliable during a deposition. And too crazy. Somehow, Glenda got word that she was being named in the divorce suit, and she was over the moon about it. Absolutely thrilled. She bragged about it to my friend, Bette, who worked at the jail. Bette, in utter disbelief, told me about Glenda's reaction to being named in a divorce case. Gladys, on the other hand proved to be easy to find, and easy to serve with papers.

Gladys Cootye's deposition was to be held two weeks from the date of service by the processors. I was so, so nervous, I don't know why. My cousin, Alma, took the day off from her job so that she could be around for me. We were going to go to lunch after the deposition, although I wasn't so sure that I would have much of an appetite. I was in the car with Alma, headed to Charlie's office, here in town, where the deposition was to be held, when I received a call from Alan. A very putout Alan informed me that the deposition would have to be postponed. Apparently, he had received a letter from Gladys, in the morning mail, saying that she had a backache, and wouldn't be able to come to the deposition. It was a personal letter from Gladys, not from a lawyer. She also informed Alan that the investigator's evidence wasn't true anymore, because he had said she was a blonde, and that now, her hair was brown.

Alan said, almost in disbelief, 'Swear to God, you can't make this stuff up! It's like some crazy comedy on television!' Then, he said that he would try to set something up at a later date. I had mixed feelings; I was disappointed because I wanted it to be over. Nevertheless, I was a tiny bit relieved.

I turned to Alma, and told her the news, and apologized for her having taken the day off for nothing. She smiled, and said, 'No problem! We'll go do a little shopping, and then have a great lunch.' Then she told me something that helped me feel better about myself. At this point, I had very little confidence or self-esteem left. She said, 'You know, you are very brave. When I got my divorce, I left the town where my husband lived, and the kids and I moved back home.

I had my parents here, and they helped me with everything. I could not have made it without them. But, you have had to stay in the same town with Jack and his family, and you are fighting them all by yourself. You are very brave.'

She emphasized it because I was sitting there, shaking my head.

'I don't feel very brave, I feel scared all of the time.'

She looked at me and said, 'That's what makes you so brave. You are scared, yet, you are standing up for yourself against an entire family.'

*****

Understandably, Alan was completely perplexed and blown away by the fact that Jack's mistress was so ignorant about the real world, and the law, that she thought that she could just blow off a legal subpoena with no qualms. I was amused at his frustration. And felt a little vindicated in my disdain for Jack's choice of a girlfriend.

Actually, it was insulting. A few weeks later, I received a copy of a court summons, or order, from a judge, ordering Gladys Cootye to appear before him to explain why she thought she could just blow off a deposition. It had taken a while for the judge to take action because, as always, we had to wait for a judge to cycle in. The court date was set to take place in a couple of weeks. Oh! Also. Still no discovery from Jack.

The court day had arrived. Alan had me wait in the plaintiff waiting room until he and Jack's lawyers could ascertain if Gladys would even show up. The waiting room was sunny with rows of pew-like benches. Several other people were in there for other cases, and I was entertained listening to their woes and stories, and sharing mine. I was in there for a long time. In fact, I out-stayed everyone. Finally, Alan showed up, looking like a thundercloud. He was angry because good old Gladys had been a no-show. The judge was also outraged that that woman had wasted everyone's time and money, and had the audacity to blow off a judge. The judge fined her two thousand dollars, which was probably what the day had cost in lawyers' fees. Jack and Gladys' sister, who had shown up for the hearing, had to pay it – they split the bill. The judge also wrote an order that would compel Gladys to attend the next scheduled deposition, or else she could face a year in jail and another hefty fine. This was a judge's order for a deposition, not ours.

Outside of the courthouse, the grounds were packed with friends of mine, and my sister, sitting on benches, or in cars, waiting to catch a glimpse of "that woman." They all were sorely disappointed that there was no sighting, but they did get to watch the conclave of Mallards and lawyers gathered outside, frantically discussing and assessing what had just transpired. My sister told us that the whole time that we were in the courthouse, Gladys had been driving around and around the courthouse grounds, but that she had never stopped.

Alan shook his head, and repeated what had become his mantra, 'You can't make this stuff up!'

He decided that, since he was already in town, and had some time, that we should walk over to Charlie's office, and sit in his conference room to talk about some things. So, we made some plans and discussed what would be coming up in the depositions, and also the mediation that would soon be looming before us. I told Alan that, since Jack had confessed to the relationship with the lovely Gladys, maybe we could skip the deposition. Believe it or not, I actually felt sorry for Gladys. She was pathetic, and seemed confused, and I felt bad about going any further with this. She seemed frightened and desperate, and I was taking no pleasure in this pitiful woman's distress. Alan shrugged and explained that it was now out of our hands; she had angered a judge, and the judge had ordered the deposition. So, we had to comply and have the deposition, or we would be held in contempt of court.

Then as we continued talking, Alan advised me that maybe I should start looking for full-time employment. At the time, I was working part-time in an antique store. I had already realized that Jack's "poor, poor, pitiful me" schtick might sway a judge, especially one that was new to the case. Remember, we had to take whatever judge cycled through. So, I had already started applying for jobs. I told Alan that I had applied for numerous jobs, to no avail. I was either overqualified or too old. So, I said, 'When you're my age, it's hard to find a good job, no one wants to hire a sixty-year-old woman.'

I had finally gotten a reaction from Alan, who had been buried in some paperwork. He raised his head, wide-eyed, from his files, and exclaimed, 'You are how old? Why did

I never bother to ask how old you were? You don't look anywhere near your age!'

'Thanks?' I said, not sure if it was a good thing.

He said, 'Never mind about the job. This changes everything!' Then we left the office to go our separate ways. Alan, as always, said that Emma would be in touch about the date and time of the next meeting. As I walked to my car, my cell phone rang. I answered. It was my friend, Fiona.

'Well!' she said gleefully, 'A no-show! I was watching from my car. I saw her circling around! I swear! That stinking coward! By the way, your lawyer is very good-looking!'

I smiled, 'He's married and much younger than I am.' You know, there really is nothing like life in a small town.

*****

While all of the legal shenanigans were going on, the Mallards were making life very difficult for me on the home front, on purpose, because they are petty, smallminded narcissists. Not only were they rude and cold towards me, but they also were still hoping to drive me out of the house, even though they knew that I had no desire, and no plans, to have the house. I just needed a roof over my head until the divorce was final, and I could figure out where I could live.

The first February of the separation, we had a terrible ice storm that caused a tremendous amount of damage to the oak trees in the yard. Several trees fell, and branches the size of trees were everywhere. I contacted Jack with voicemails (he wouldn't answer if I called), texts, and letters.

No response.

So, the man who helped me with the yard, another worker, and I spent six weeks working together, and cleaned up what we could. Some of the debris was too large for us as I had no type of heavy equipment. I kept trying to get in touch with Jack to let him know that several of the outbuildings were damaged.

No response.

I finally sent a letter to the Mallard law firm, and a copy to Alan. The only response I received was that they sent an adjustor over to the property.

No repair. No cleanup. No response to me.

Then the following spring, the central heat and air unit, which was ancient, began to wheeze its last breaths. I had a repairman come out, and he managed to patch it back together, but he warned me that it was a temporary fix, that the unit was on its last legs, and would more than likely break down for good before long. I let Jack know (the usual: voicemails, texts, letters).

No response. So, so typical.

Now, we will take a peek even further in the past, pre-separation. Jack and I lived in this house that was jointly owned by Jack and his brothers, and their heirs. They, including Jack, never fixed anything on the house, except once in twenty-three years, they all paid to have the exterior painted. Over the years, the roof began to leak everywhere. Every time it rained, I had to run around the house, placing coolers, buckets, pots, and bowls all over the house. Then the leaks began to run into the walls and bookcases. Jack did nothing, neither did his brothers. Also, the columns, window sills, porch balustrades (upstairs and downstairs), and the porch floor were rotten. So, I spent most of my inheritance and salary fixing up a house that would never be mine. Once again, I know, groan. What a fool, but a very nice fool. Why would I do this? Because it was the right thing to do. The house was a beauty, and to let it crumble away was almost criminal, and disrespectful to the memory of my mother-in-law and father-in-law. Here is a partial list of what I did to help Jack look responsible in front of his brothers. I paid for a new roof, new handmade columns, and one hundred forty-three new balustrades; I rebuilt the front porch, rescreened the back porch, and replaced various windows and window sills. Also, I redid the hardwood floors, remodeled the kitchen and master bedroom, and repainted the entire interior (twice). I also kept the huge yard up by paying someone to help me every Friday; we worked together. Once a year, I would hire a landscaping company to come in and completely clean the whole five acres. That made it easier for me and my helper to keep it up the rest of the year. Although I could go on and on, this gives you a good idea of the fact that I always pulled my weight, and I always tried to be a productive part of the family.

So, now, back to the time of the separation and the central heat and air. The first week in July that year, I had to have sinus surgery. When I got home from the surgery, the central heat and air unit had expired. I spent the weekend with fans encircling me. Southern summers are very hot and humid. And I felt perfectly awful after the surgery. The repressive heat made me feel even worse. The repairman came out and tried to revive the unit by replacing several parts. This went on for several weeks. It was miserable! Finally, the repairman announced, very apologetically, that the unit was dead. I began a campaign of voicemails, texts, and letters to Jack.

No response.

Most of the windows in the house had been painted shut for decades, so they couldn't be opened to get fresh air and maybe a breeze in the house. I went upstairs and got a small window unit I had installed in the master bedroom (Jack would not let me turn on the central heat and air unit until it was ninety degrees in the bedroom, hence the window unit). I found a window in the guestroom that would open, and installed the window unit there. I closed off the rest of the house, and lived in the guest bedroom and bath, the den, and the kitchen.

Never a word or response from the Mallards.

So, in August, at the mediation, I mentioned my dilemma to Alan, and explained that I did not want to buy a new central heat and air unit for a house that was not mine, and would never be mine. He agreed, and mentioned it to the Mallards sometime during the long day.

No response.

In October, the temperatures plummeted, and we had an unusually cold October. I now lived in the den and kitchen, and opened the door to the dining room so that I could use the gas logs. I slept on the sofa. I also had a large electric heater. The temperature in the rest of the house was forty-two degrees. I took a picture of the thermometer in the living room. I finally called Alan. He was livid! He had thought that the Mallards had rectified the problem. I explained to him that I had been sending voicemails, texts, and letters to Jack, for months, with no response. Alan made some calls and got us an emergency hearing with a judge for the next week. For once, we lucked out and a judge had just cycled in. Since we had moved so quickly, Jack and just one lawyer attended the hearing. The judge was absolutely appalled and also livid. He ordered the Mallards to replace the unit. Three weeks later, I had heat, and it was sublime. Best of all, the Mallards had failed in their attempt to force me out of the house. At the same time, it helped to reveal to the rest of the town the pettiness and bullying mentality of the Mallards. It was a very small victory, but a victory nonetheless!

Chapter Nine

There were legal activities taking place concurrent with the home-front dilemmas. August had rolled around, and it was time for our mediation. What a farce and waste of time! Except it did give me insight into the mindset of the Mallards, and it definitely wasn't "warm and fuzzy" towards me. This was surprisingly crushing to me because I am a consummate people-pleaser, and I always want people to like me, but I should have expected this. However, I was beginning to get used to their cruelty. In fact, I was standing my ground, and proving to be much more of an adversary than anyone, me included, had expected.

Mediation was to start at nine o'clock in the morning, at a neutral law office, in the big city. I didn't know what to expect, so I was almost breathless with anxiety. But, I did look cute in a darling, blue sundress, and ready to do battle. I arrived before Alan, but the mediating lawyer quickly showed me to a small conference room, where I was alone. It turned out that the Mallards and their enclave had already assembled in a larger conference room across the hall. Either there just plain wasn't enough room for me to cram into the main conference room, or Tom, the mediator, realized that he couldn't, in good conscience, put me into the buzzing, humming nest of angry hornets that the Mallards embodied.

So, I sat quietly alone. A secretary had kindly brought me a bottle of water, and I sat and wrote endless to-do lists in a notebook that I had brought with me. Then the door flew open, and Alan had arrived! I felt stronger and more confident as soon as I saw his bright, intelligent, blue eyes and his big smile.

'Guess what?' he exclaimed, 'Jack finally brought his discovery!' He stood back as several people paraded in and out, depositing boxes and boxes of files. We both stood looking at them with raised eyebrows, and expressions that said, "Whew!" Then Tom entered the room, and he and Alan discussed how the activities of the day would play out. Tom, of course, was to be a neutral courier between the two conference rooms, relaying offers, suggestions, and demands from one room to the other. They felt that it would be counterproductive and cruel to make me sit in the room with the angry clan. And so, we spent the day in the most tedious waste of time and energy I have ever experienced – nine and a half hours of it!

Back and forth. Back and forth. The poor mediator spent most of his time in the hornet's nest. We had a break for lunch with sandwiches and soft drinks being furnished. We had to eat our lunch in the conference room. About midafternoon, Tom walked into our conference room. Alan and I were kicked back, laughing, and chatting.

Tom leaned on our table, and said, 'I know I'm supposed to be neutral here, but those are the worst people I have ever worked with!' He told us that if Jack could have been here without his brothers, we might have gotten something accomplished. He said that when he would bring something up, that Jack would listen and nod, but then his brothers would leap in and clear the room, making everyone leave, even the lawyers. Then they would browbeat Jack until he bent to their way of thinking.

'This,' Tom explained, 'is what is dragging this out and making it such an ordeal.' He even said that it was a good thing that we were not in the same room with them; he honestly didn't think that he could control those angry little despots.

Now, know that I wasn't asking for much: a down payment on a house and some type of allowance to help with mortgage, insurance, and tax payments which I wasn't used to paying. Neither was Jack (the company owned by all of the brothers had always paid all of that from timber sales). A little after six o'clock, Tom entered the room with their final offer of the day. Remember, I had been a productive, contributing, kind, supportive part of that family for decades. I even diapered their parents. The final offer was a one-time settlement of fifty thousand dollars, I could keep my Toyota, and they wanted my jewelry back.

My mouth dropped open, I looked at Tom, and said, 'I can keep my car? Why, of course I can! I paid for that car with my own money! And the jewelry? All of the jewelry were gifts!' I should have added that it was just jewelry, not the Crown Jewels.

Tom didn't look surprised, he said, 'Well, there seems to be one ring in particular.'

I interrupted quickly with, 'A gift! No deal!'

Alan looked at Tom, smiled kindly and tiredly, and said, 'Tom, you have done a remarkable job today in an impossible situation. I don't know how you have kept your cool with those people over there. I'm sorry that we have wasted your time. The offer is unacceptable. I can't believe that, after over nine hours that is all that they could come up with. It's time to go home. Tell them that we will see them in court.'

Tom agreed. Alan told Tom that he would send someone over the next day to collect Jack's discovery, and we left. Alan squeezed my shoulder, and, as usual, 'Emma will call you tomorrow to set up a meeting.'

I asked, 'What do we do next?'

He smiled, 'We hold some depositions, and then we go to court.'

It was a long drive back home that evening. I   think that I cried the whole way. I don't know if it was tears of exhaustion, frustration, or an all-consuming sadness that we had come to this. Or maybe it was the gut-wrenching pain of knowing that I was so insignificant to those people that they would insult me with their ridiculous offer. But they had done me a favor: after I was all cried out, I realized that I was going to have to cast away all feelings of loyalty, love, and sadness for those people, that I really was alone in this, that a standoff was imminent, and that I was going to have to take care of me! Come hell or high water!

*****

We returned to the mundane reality of divorce. All was quiet for the holidays again, and once again, I received the usual telephone calls and paperwork. Then the Mallards must have decided that it was time to take a small revenge on me, or so they thought. Around the beginning of January, I received an order for discovery for me. The Mallards wanted my discovery by February 28, and wanted my telephone, bank, and credit card records for the past ten years. Obviously, they were trying to get even for the ordeal Jack had made of gathering his information. He did it all from his own endless boxes, cabinets, and drawers of files, and word has it that he burned up his copier making endless copies, and because he is anal: copies of copies. Calmly, I made a few calls, paid some nominal fees, and had everything I needed from all of the institutions and companies in less than ten days. I triumphantly took them to Alan, who had them delivered to Jack's main lawyer. I told Alan to be sure and let Jack and his brothers know that it had been a cinch and absolutely no problem.

Then I received a copy of the order for Gladys Cootye's deposition. It was to be held at Charlie's office, here in town, the first week in February. Alan had also lined up depositions with land and timber managers, who handled most of the Mallards' land holdings, for the same day. It promised to be a very exhausting and emotionally draining day!

The day of reckoning was upon us. The depositions of the land and timber managers were to be first, and then Gladys Cootye was scheduled for eleven o'clock. When I arrived, Alan, as usual, had not gotten there yet. But the Mallards had! In full force! But with just one lawyer. They had obviously pared the legal convention down to one, but it was the best one: Mr. McDonald. Actually, it was not mandatory that they, or their lawyer, be present. However, by now, you know how the Mallards are. A secretary put me in Charlie's office to wait on Alan. He showed up, right on time. The conference room was small. A court reporter sat at the head of the table. At these depositions, only the lawyer and the person being deposed speak. One at a time, the people being deposed sat to the right of the court reporter. Then there was Mr. McDonald with Jack next to him. One of the brothers sat at the end of the table, and one sat on my side of the table, one space away from me. It definitely was a roomful. These depositions were cut and dried numbers and facts, boring and a little over my head. We took a brief break, and then it was time for the star attraction, The Mistress.

At the time, I didn't know that my sister was camped out in front of the law office, which was in a charming old house with a lovely yard. My sister was determined to get a picture of good old Gladys so our friends could know what she looked like. Everyone was curious. I had mixed feelings about photographing Gladys, and had told my sister the day before not to do it. I felt sorry for Gladys. She seemed such a poor, old thing. I just couldn't take any pleasure in any of this. However, afterwards, I was fine with the fact that she had snapped a few pictures. They turned out to be a source of intense interest and shock for our friends. Neither I nor my friends could understand Jack's attraction to this unfortunate creature.

Alan and I were back in our seats, after the break, when there was a commotion in the lobby. Gladys had arrived with her nasty sister and a lawyer in tow. Because of the room constraints, Jack's brothers were not allowed into the conference room. They had to wait in the lobby, so I am sure that they got a shocking eyeful when Gladys, Jack's paramour, walked in. Gladys, her mangy sister, and the lawyer sat opposite me and Alan. Mr. McDonald was at the end of the table, and Jack was on my side of the table, a chair width from me. It was an uncomfortable, eerie sensation to have him sitting silently almost next to me.

When I looked at Gladys Cootye for the first time in over twenty years, I felt a pang of pity for her, life had not been kind to her. Her hair was badly dyed a light pinkish brown, and tied in an on-the-side ponytail. She was short and dumpy, almost puffy, and she had miles and miles of wrinkles. She looked scared to death. And I felt bad for her. I turned to Alan. My expression must have said, "Please, let's don't," because he held up his hand and said softly, 'We have to.'

I don't know where they found their lawyer, but this must have been one of his first cases. Gladys looked stunned and petrified as she gave the court reporter her name, birthdate, and address. She looked so scared and confused that I felt my heart squeeze up with pity. I felt sorry for her pain and fear.

Then when Alan began to question Gladys, her rube lawyer jumped in, and shushed her, saying to Alan, 'I have advised my client to take the fifth on the grounds that she may incriminate herself.'

Alan sat for a second or two, blinking, I am sure he was trying to figure out what he was going to say without making the lawyer look foolish. Finally, Alan said, 'Sir, we don't have a judge here, we just have someone here to record what is said. There will be no arrests or punishment for anything that is said. It is not a hearing. It's just questions and answers.'

The lawyer stubbornly repeated, 'I am advising my client to take the fifth on the grounds that she may incriminate herself.'

Alan took a deep breath, and calmly said, 'Sir, this is, as you are aware, just a civil case. You do realize that every time she invokes the Fifth Amendment, it will be recorded as a "yes." The judge will receive copies of these depositions.' The lawyer mulishly repeated his statement. Alan shrugged, looked at me with an expression that said, 'My God, only in a small town,' and began his questioning. He framed his questions so that "yes" was the answer we needed. It didn't take long, just long enough to confirm that Gladys had had a long sexual relationship with Jack, knowing that he was married, and that she had received some financial help from him. I sat, mesmerized, watching her, wondering how Jack could have even wanted to be with her, and yet, feeling sorry for her. I was also keenly aware of Jack sitting still and silent next to me. I wondered what he was thinking. He had to be embarrassed. After we had gathered all the damning material we needed, the deposition was called to an end. We all collected our things, and stood to leave. As I rose and turned, Jack was doing the same, and we were standing eye to eye. I had not spoken in person or on the telephone to Jack in almost two years.

I couldn't help it, I murmured to him, 'You should be ashamed of yourself.'

Jack jerked upright and then leaned forward into my face, and screamed, 'I should be ashamed? You should be ashamed! You are financially ruining both of us!'

Alan quickly stepped between us, and Mr. McDonald pulled Jack away. Alan and I waited until Jack had been shuttled out, then we waited for the crowd to disperse before we exited the building. Alan said, 'I'll have Emma call you tomorrow to set up a meeting. You might not think so, but it all went well. See, it wasn't so bad.' I nodded, and stepped out the front door onto the open porch. My sister was perched there, smiling, holding up her camera. I waved and grinned. There's nothing like a sister!

*****

A few weeks later, I had a voicemail from Emma, and all she said was, 'I want you to know that your tapes are a powerful weapon.' Finally! They must have gotten the transcripts. It was too late to call that day, but I called her early the next morning. She repeated her recorded message that the tapes were a powerful weapon. Then she told me about the man who had prepared the transcripts and delivered them to the office. Emma said that, as he handed her the tapes and transcripts, he had said, 'You know, I've been doing this for a living for over twenty years.'

Emma said that she nodded, while thinking, *Oh, my God, he's going to tell me that he ruined the tapes!*

Then he said, 'You know that I've heard it all. I want you to know that these are the worst that I've ever heard, and I'm not talking about the quality. I have never, in my entire life, heard a man talk to another human being, much less his wife, the way this man talks to that poor woman! My only hope is that that poor woman is your client, and that she gets everything she deserves!' I thanked Emma for telling me; I felt vindicated.

Then Emma told me that now the Mallards wanted me to list all the furniture in the house. They wanted me to make two columns, one for me and the other for Jack, and then list the furniture, room by room, designating to whom each piece belonged. So, I did. Not only did I list the furniture, but I also listed and designated rugs, lamps, and paintings. I was meticulous, careful, and honest. Then I made a special trip to the city to take the lists to Alan's office. Alan then forwarded copies of the list to Mr. McDonald. A few days later, Alan called me. Absolutely disgusted with the Mallards. When they had received the furniture list, they had gone ballistic, demanding to know what had happened to Jack's silver and "Mother's china." I think that they were implying that I had stolen or sold Jack's things. The nerve of those people! I hadn't, but I wish I had thought of that – just kidding. Alan reminded Mr. McDonald that the request had been for furniture only, and that I had complied immediately and had gone the extra mile by doing more than they asked me to do.

Mr. McDonald agreed and explained this to the Mallards. I even offered to make lists of the silver, china, and crystal, as well as knick knacks. But nothing would suit these bullies but a walk-through of the house to make sure, personally, that everything was there. Alan told Mr. McDonald that he would set it up, and be back in touch.

Good Lord! Was there no end to the insulting denigration and sense of entitlement of these people? I could not wait to be finally and completely free of these pompous, puffed-up, self-important bullies.

*****

A few weeks after the brouhaha over the furniture list, I got a call from Alan. He said that the Mallards were adamant about the walk-through. They wanted to walk through the house to see how it was, and to see if Jack's things were still there. I could actually see their point; after all, it was their house. But I resented their attitude and implications. Alan asked if I felt okay with them coming to the house, and would I be comfortable being face-to-face, alone with them. I told Alan that I would be fine with Jack and his lawyer.

'No, no lawyers,' Alan said, 'the Mallards, all of them. Jack and his brothers. And the wives are insisting that they be allowed to come too.'

I gasped; my stomach sank. I told him that there was no way that I could be there alone, and so vulnerable, with that crowd. Alan agreed, and suggested that I find someone who would be comfortable with them, and not confrontational, and see if he, or she, would house-sit while the Mallards walked around the house.

I asked my cousin, Alma, who is no-nonsense, strong, fearless, and level-headed, if she would do this for me. She said that she would be delighted to do it. So, Alan firmed up a date, and established the parameters, to which they all agreed. He said that they would be allowed one hour in the house and on the grounds, and that they could not plunder, or look through cabinets, closets, and drawers. Which, of course, is exactly what they did.

The day and night before the walk-through, I feverishly scrubbed, dusted, polished, washed, and mopped the entire house. The morning of the walkthrough, I packed up all of my house animals, the dogs and a couple of old cats, into my car. I didn't want them underfoot, or to possibly have an accident, with these people there. Several of my friends had suggested that I do this, so the Mallards wouldn't complain about the animals, or possibly mistreat them. I figured that I could drive around for an hour. After all, what's an hour?

The night before, I had also gotten all of the china and silver out. I arranged it in several different sections; silver that Jack inherited from his parents was on the sideboard, silver I inherited from my parents was on a drop-leaf table, along with my silver chest (with my mother's initials on it), that contained my mother's silver. I had arranged Jack's mother's china on one end of the dining room table, and my mother's china on the other end. In the middle of the table, I placed the silver and china that we had received as wedding presents, which I thought that we would probably split. I had labels at each section, explaining what everything was.

In addition, I left instructions with Alma explaining the arrangement. I also explained that I had all the oriental rugs professionally cleaned, but that one in the library had suffered when the roof leaked, and the rug company had declared it hopelessly ruined and had thrown it out. I also explained that some of the books were missing because they, too, were ruined during the roof leaks. Then I explained that some of Mr. Mallard's "valuable" Time/Life collections had been packed up years ago and stored in the attic. I did not know how picky they were going to be, but I wanted to cover all bases. But Jack had been here during all of the roof damage, so he could also corroborate what I had written.

So, that morning, after Alma had arrived, the animals and I went for a leisurely, air conditioned drive around the county. After the ordained hour, I returned. They were still there. Cars all over the yard. I pulled into my neighbors' cool, shady yard across the street, got out of the car, and walked to their front door. It opened before I could knock. My neighbor handed me an extra pair of binoculars, and motioned for me to come in. We stood at the window and watched the show across the street. The Mallards were all over the house and yard like flies, carrying clipboards. Every now and then, one would drive off, and then come back with a new handful of papers. They had been there for almost four hours when I finally called Emma. The animals had been watered, and were cool and comfortable, but they were restless, and come on, enough is enough. Alan was at an out of town deposition, but Emma texted him. Alan was irate, and called Mr. McDonald, who was also angry, with his clients. Mr. McDonald called the Mallards, and told them that they had to abide by the agreement, and that it was past time for them to leave. They reluctantly did. And my poor animals could finally go home and stretch their legs.

When I entered the house and thanked Alma, she, too, was angry about the behavior of the Mallards. She said that she had repeatedly told them not to go through things, and reminded them that they were to just walk around. They blatantly and arrogantly ignored her, and opened and inspected every cabinet, chest, closet, and drawer in the house. Even my underwear drawer (why am I not surprised about that?). Alma then told me that Myrna Rae had practically pushed her over so that she could go through my silver chest, spoon by spoon, fork by fork. She finally found a spoon with an S on it, and had gleefully announced that it must belong to the Mallards since they had some obscure ancestor whose last name began with an S. Thank God for family! Alma squared up to her, and reminded Myrna Rae that my grandmother's maiden name began with an S. So, that was that.

Alma was shocked at what grasping, petty people the Mallards were. Before they left, Bob had told Alma that they needed at least six more hours in the house, and that they would like to come back the next day. Alma had texted me, and I had then relayed everything to Emma, and thus Alan, who had immediately called Mr. McDonald. Alan told Mr. McDonald, 'She has done everything that they have asked – and more. Enough is enough! They are just trying to run over her. So, not only no, but hell no!'

Mr. McDonald agreed, and apologized for his rude clients and their boorish behavior. So, now I was one step closer to the end of this circus. I still had a ways to go, but the end was almost in sight. Next, we had our depositions looming on the horizon.

Chapter Ten

Our depositions were definitely the climax of this sad tale of woe. Everything else was either the setup or the denouement. A week or so before my and Jack's depositions, I met with Alan and Emma to go over possible questions that Mr. McDonald might ask, and questions that Alan should ask Jack. Once again, Alan explained to me that depositions were just questions and answers with no judge present. I was a little puzzled about why he was telling me this again, after all, I had already been present at several depositions.

But then he clarified what he was trying to tell me: 'When Mr. McDonald asks you a question, you make sure that you answer it, but since there is no judge to control how much, and what, is said, you can insert a lot more information that you want on the record.'

Ohhh…hmm…

He also reminded me that when Jack was being questioned, I could, of course, be present, but that I had to remain silent, 'No matter how hard it is, or what is said.'

Then Alan pulled a stack of papers out of his desk, and said, 'Your brothers-in-law faxed this to me. It's forty-eight pages. What in the world is it?'

Curious, I picked up the wad of pages. Good Lord! It was the original list of everything Mr. and Mrs. Mallard, my in-laws, had left in the house decades ago for their four boys. It was the list that the Mallard brothers had used when they divided their parents' personal property. If you studied the list, you could see initials beside each item, indicating which brother had inherited or selected that item. I looked up at Alan and explained what it was.

I cannot describe how exasperated he looked, 'What am I supposed to do with this?'

I looked at him and shrugged, then shaking my head, I explained that it was a useless list because all of the items had been dispersed, except for Jack's one-fourth, which was still in the house. And I had already made a list of those for them. I said, 'Maybe they want you to compare what is Jack's on that list with what I listed.'

Alan gave me an eye roll and a sideways look, and said, 'He's already signed off on your list, and agreed to the wedding present division. This is just more of their interfering garbage. But your brother-in-law, Bob, on the cover sheet, asked about a tablecloth.' He showed me the page on which Bob had scrawled, "Where is Elise Willis' great-aunt Lizzie's tablecloth?"

Elise Willis, a close friend of Jack's parents, had died somewhere around 1942, so I had no idea about the tablecloth. I said, 'Swear to God, Alan, I have absolutely no idea what he is talking about.' Then it dawned on me, I did have an answer to the mystery. After Mrs. Mallard's death, it took the brothers over two years to divide up the property, and then another year to move the things they had inherited from the house in which Jack and I were living. They finally moved everything when I got up the nerve to tell them that I refused to be the curator of the Mallard Museum anymore, and that, if they didn't get their things, I would move them to the outbuilding where my family things were moldering, and then I'd move my things in. Jack's brother, Mark had inherited the linen chest. The brothers had never bothered to go through anything in the house, so as they came to get the large pieces of furniture, I had to clean them out, and put the items into boxes that I labeled with the name of the piece of furniture and the room from which it had come. Then I put the boxes in a weatherized storage room, thinking that they would go through them later. The full boxes are still where I put them. I had somehow forgotten to clear out the linen chest, and Mark had driven off with the chest and the linens. I had immediately called Myrna Rae, who had called Ed, who was to call Mark. I figured my part in this was over.

I explained this whole convoluted story to Alan, and told him that the brothers needed to ask Mark's children about great-aunt Lizzie's tablecloth. Alan smiled weakly, and said, 'I'm so tired of those people. This table cloth is neither important nor pertinent. If anyone asks again, I'll relay the story. Otherwise, let's just forget about it.'

Then I asked Alan that, since it was my deposition, could I choose to, for once, not have Jack's brothers present. Alan looked at me, 'Of course, you can. But,' he leaned forward and smiled, 'for once, I think that you might want to have them there.' Reluctantly, I agreed to it. After the deposition, all I could think was that, *Wow! Was he ever right! Thank you, Alan.*

*****

The depositions were held the first week in May in Alan's firm's conference room. Because of the distance, Mr. McDonald and one of the brothers had to travel, the depositions were set to begin at one o'clock in the afternoon. I wore a madras shift, espadrilles, and because I was feeling a little spunky, I wore some cute, dangly, artsy earrings. I was ready! Alan had me in his office for a pep talk.

He said, 'Remember, this is your chance. Anything you want to get in, get it in. You say whatever you want, but tell the truth!'

I looked at Alan, 'Of course I'll tell the truth. I always tell the truth. My mother always said that nothing fits like the truth!'

Then we rose and walked into the conference room. It was the usual arrangement: court reporter at the head of the table, the two camps on either side. When we were being questioned, Jack and I would change seats with our lawyers so that we could be directly across from the lawyer asking us questions. Luckily, Jack was up first, and Alan led him through a labyrinth of questions. Jack was angry. He was beet-red and haughty, with a huge chip on his shoulder. He tried to tear me down at every opportunity. I was feeling a little sorry for him... And then! He said that I had been unfaithful, and that, at the time, he had forgiven me. I shot up like a bullet, and squeaked, 'That's a lie!'

Alan grabbed my hand and whispered, 'No talking. Address it later.' You better believe I was going to address it. (However, I don't know why I was so shocked, Jack used to accuse me of being with other men constantly – no doubt, his own guilty conscience.) I scribbled Alan a note: 'Find out when, where, and circumstances; I am going to let him hang himself.' Alan asked all the right questions. When I heard Jack's response, I knew I had him, this would be a cinch. I was chomping at the bit for my turn. By now, it was hard to take Jack's whining and anger and lies. It was actually good for me to witness this. No second thoughts now!

After a brief break for powder rooms and water, it was my turn. I couldn't wait! I calmly answered the name and address rigmaroles. As soon as there was an opening, I jumped in.

'I want to address Jack's crazy accusation about me.' I provided all the real details that proved that this had taken place in 1979, not the 1994 that he tried to say it was. Good Lord, I was diapering Jack's mother in 1994, and we weren't married until 1992. I had all the evidence that was needed to blow his alcohol-confused lie out of the water; as a onetime favor for a fellow teacher, I had agreed to chaperone the high school Radio Club at the local radio station so that they could tape their weekly radio show. The teacher who sponsored them had to attend a meeting, so I helped out. Jack, for years, kept accusing me of having met someone out there, because I had never mentioned chaperoning this group before. I had to listen to this sad accusation for almost forty years.

Then Mr. McDonald broke what I had always heard was the first rule that a lawyer learned: never ask a question to which you don't already know the answer. Mr. McDonald fixed his big blue eyes on me, and asked, 'Well, Mrs. Mallard, if what your husband said isn't true, why do you think he said it?' I couldn't believe he was opening this can of worms!

I smiled at Mr. McDonald, and looking into his eyes, said, 'I honestly don't know, Mr. McDonald, probably for the same reason that he said I had sex with my dogs, and his brothers, and just about every man in the county! It's all on the tapes!'

Mr. McDonald looked dumfounded. Out of the comer of my eye, I could see that Alan looked pleased. Mr. McDonald looked at Alan, and then back at me, and said, 'I haven't had a chance to listen to the tapes yet.' Then Mr. McDonald said, 'Tell me about the tapes.'

Oh. My. God! Really? And so, I did. If he thought that I was going to tell some story about hidden, secret tapes that he could get thrown out of court, he was sadly mistaken. I told him about buying the tape recorder, and why. Then I explained that I always showed the recorder to Jack, and always had it out in the open on a table for him to see.

I stole a sneak peek down the table. Jack's oldest brother was so pale that even his lips looked white. I realized then that Jack had never told them the truth of what had really happened between us. Too bad. Jack looked like a thundercloud. He had a look of cold, furious hatred on his face. I figured that we weren't going to ever be friends again after this. Then Mr. McDonald changed his line of questioning. He asked question after question about the "alleged" physical abuse, each time getting me to admit that I had not gone to the police, and that there were no pictures of any bruises. Then, he asked about Jack grabbing me by the neck, and did his usual buildup to "no pictures." I went right along with him then, 'No, no pictures,' then, 'but you can hear it on the tape.'

Mr. McDonald looked at Alan, and then back at me, nodded, and said, 'I definitely need to listen to those tapes.'

Mr. McDonald motioned for me to continue. We locked eyes almost like lovers. From then on, I was unstoppable, and Mr. McDonald let me run with it. I waxed lyrical about the abuse; Jack's alcoholism, how I had, to no avail, reached out to his family. I described my relationship with Jack's parents, and how I had taken care of them. I went into great detail about Mrs. Mallard's dementia, and how I somehow became the primary caregiver. I described the work I had done to the house. I told him about how I had tried to give Jack a chance to come clean, with Bob and Trudy right there in the car with us. I described his seamy, sordid relationships with Glenda and Gladys. I left no stone unturned. Oh, my God! I was on fire!

When I was finished, I tore my eyes from Mr. McDonald's and looked down the table. Jack's brothers looked like death warmed over. I was afraid that we might have to call the EMS. Jack looked stunned and absolutely furious! I think that if someone had pulled on his finger, steam would have come out of his nose and ears! They all said, almost in unison, that they needed to take a break. The Mallard camp and lawyer exited the conference room, leaving me with Emma, Alan, and the poor court reporter.

Everyone was quiet for a few minutes. Then Emma grinned, and said, 'Wow!'

Alan nodded, then grinned, and said, 'Mm-mmm! You done good!' The court reporter stood and gave me a thumbs up. Before anyone could say anything else, a secretary poked her head into the conference room, and addressing Alan, said that Mr. McDonald wanted to speak to him. Alan raised his eyebrows and left. Emma went to get us some water, and I was left in blessed silence.

A few minutes later, Alan came back into the conference room, almost walking on air. First, he said, almost in surprise, 'Mr. McDonald really likes you. He said that he thinks that the Mallards will be making a serious offer within the next few days. He said that they definitely do not want this to go to court.' I was speechless. It was really happening! God is good! I was going to be alright! Then Alan told me that Emma would call me tomorrow. Well, you know the drill.

I thanked Emma and Alan, gathered my things, and left. It was seven forty-five, another very long day. As I passed the receptionist (who had stayed late), I smiled and said good night. She grinned and called out, 'Way to go! They looked like they had their tails between their legs!' I laughed and waved goodbye. Then I walked to my car and drove home. I didn't shed a single tear the whole way home.

Later that night, long after I had gotten home, the phone rang. It was Annie. She was bubbling with excitement. She said that Charlie had gone to a Bar Association meeting after work, and had bumped into Alan there. Obviously, Alan had not gone straight home after the depositions. He must have needed a drink after another long day with the Mallards. Annie said that Charlie had asked Alan if we had had the depositions, and if so, how had they gone. Alan had grinned, lifted his drink in a toast, and announced, 'She was a f*****g rock star!'

Chapter Eleven

Well, Alan's insight into Mr. McDonald's statements was
spot on: The Mallards were very definitely afraid of going
to court. Three weeks after the depositions, we were in our
final divorce hearing, a private hearing before a judge, with
no locals sitting in and listening, which is what would have
happened had this gone to court. For the first time during
this entire, exhausting divorce, it was as it should have been:
just me and my lawyer, and Jack and his lawyer. I had spent
the entire two years fighting an entire family. This hearing
was just a formality, we had already reached a settlement.
All we had to do was to agree to everything in front of a
judge, and then it was over. Kind of a letdown after all the
hoopla in the past. Jack would pay for a house for me, not
just a down payment, and I was to receive a nice settlement,
some property, alimony, and Jack would pay all of the very
sizeable attorneys' fees. Not bad! I certainly wasn't going
to be rich, but I was going to be A.O.K., which is all I had
asked for in the first place.

While we were in the courtroom, Jack refused to even
acknowledge me, but I, for once, didn't care. This man and
his clan had tried their best to break me, and I had emerged
bent, but unbroken; bruised, but unbowed. When I left the

courthouse that day, I never looked back. I gave Alan a big hug when we were outside. The separation anxiety must have shown on my face, because he assured me that we would still be in touch for a few months until everything was in place, and things were going smoothly. As he strode off to his car, I wanted to run after him like a lost or abandoned puppy. I stood for a minute, feeling lost and empty. Then I took a deep breath of the sweet scent of spring and freedom, and walked to my car. It was time to start my life again – my way. It was time to rediscover me, if I could even find me.

*****

Now, I know that, after you have invested so much time in reading about this part of my life, you surely want to know what happened to me. Well, I found a beautiful house on the golf course, and it has a large, lovely yard for my beasts. I have great neighbors around me. My wonderful friends visit often. The house is open and bright with French doors and windows drawing sunshine and life inside. One of my dear friends, who used to be an interior decorator and now owns a lovely antique store, offered to help me arrange my furniture and hang pictures. I had all of my chairs and sofas recovered in beautiful silk and linen fabrics – some light and floral, some bright yellow, and some cream-colored. I also had an awesome art collection, most of which I had inherited. My friend stood in the middle of the living room, looking around to decide what to put where. He turned to me, smiling, and said, 'You know, whenever you come into my store, you always have on a crisp linen sundress, and you always have a big smile on your face. We are going to keep this house open, and bright, and airy. Just perfect for someone who wears crisp dresses and big smiles.' He was as good as his word, my house is beautiful and comfortable, and so, so peaceful.

*****

One day, when I was at work, I looked out the front window, and who was standing there, admiring the flowers, but Glenda. Egad! I stood frozen, almost like a startled deer. Should I step back so that she couldn't see me? Or should I hold my ground and be nice? Well, you know me well enough by now to know what I did. I met her eyes, through the glass, and smiled, and raised my hand in greeting. Poor thing! She lit up like a Christmas tree and rushed into the store to talk to me. I had decided that it was no use to be angry with this poor creature who had been cruelly exploited and used. As she approached me, she began to apologize for what all had happened. I held up my hand to stop her apologies, and told her that I didn't care about it, and that I didn't blame her. I said that it wasn't her fault, that she had been used. I hope some of it took root, but she wasn't really listening, she was too busy giving me an explanation that I didn't really want to hear. She wanted to apologize for the pictures.

She said, 'Jack paid me fifty dollars to let him take those pictures. I don't know why he kept them on his phone so long. I told him that those pictures would come back to bite us both in the butt! But he said that he likes to look at them in the mornings and play with himself.'

Thank you, Glenda, for a mental picture and memory I will never be able to forget. How disgustingly sick and nasty, and deplorable! Oh, well, it is what it is! At least it helped to reinforce the knowledge that I was better off without that Triple A (abusive alcoholic adulterer) jerk in my life, and that it was time to forge and follow a new path to a new life.

*****

My new life was peaceful and rejuvenating, however, even though I became more and more like my old self, I still had not rekindled my old sense of joy and fun. Remember, when I was young, I was the belly flopping family clown. I had been invited to a bridal shower for my younger sister's future daughter-in-law. Although showers are really not my thing, of course, I would attend. It was family. I was to pick my sister up so that we could go together. Enroute to my sister's house, while listening to a favorite CD – yes, I'm old – I began to think about advice and lessons learned that I wish I could pass on to someone. Since I am childless, I will pass it on to you!

Be kind, it's so easy to do, and is less trouble and takes less energy than being mean. Feed a dog, feed a cat, and then, why not give them a home. They will return your love in spades, and mean it. Every so often, watch a sad movie, and cry your eyes out. It is cleansing. Then watch a funny movie, and laugh out loud until your sides hurt, and your heart smiles. Remember to feed the birds. In fact, feed any of God's creatures that need a helping hand. Don't whine and complain; make "getting by" look easy. Always help turtles across the road. Read lots of good books, often, and over and over. Let someone out in traffic, or let someone ahead of you in the grocery line; you will not only make their day, but yours as well. Don't hold grudges. The other person wins if you do, and besides, it's too exhausting. Lastly, never walk by something that is not right, and do nothing (this explains the number of pets I have).

*****

I pulled into my sister's yard; she climbed into the car, and directed me to the shower. When we pulled into our destination, I realized that it was a church fellowship hall. Uh-oh. However, I was from a Presbyterian background where wine was often permitted at communion and other functions in the fellowship hall. I voiced my optimistic view to my sister, who dashed my hopes, with raised eyebrows and the whisper, 'They're Baptists!' Oh, well.

Everyone at the shower was very nice. And after we had endured sitting in a circle to play parlor games, and watch the bride-to-be open gifts, the ladies urged me, as the visiting guest, to start the line for refreshments. Strangely, the table was on a raised stage. I had to climb several steps to get to it. I perused the table, laden with food, and decided that the food looked delish. But the two punch bowls, filled with liquid, looked a little suspect: one was an unappetizing, pale pink concoction, and the other appeared to be urine. I looked down over the crowd; I was still the only one on the stage. They turned their faces up toward me. Oh my God! This was my moment! I smiled out over the crowd, and exclaimed, 'My goodness! Everything looks wonderful!'

My eyes met my sister's beautiful, blue mischievous eyes, and she grinned. At that moment, I felt a small surge of energy, like a small spark had ignited in my heart. I spread my arms out, smiled, and asked, 'So, which one of these is the spiked punch?' My sister and some of the younger set laughed, the rest didn't get it. But that was perfectly all right. Because that spark that I felt was not heartburn, it was that missing part of me coming back to life. I had finally found me again. I felt whole again. I wanted to strike a strongman victory pose, instead, I calmly and quietly sipped a cup of urine.

My sister and I giggled all the way back to her house. After I dropped her off, I headed home to my beautiful, peaceful, sunny house, and my beloved dogs and cats. As I drove, my mind wandered back to my advice, this time to myself as well. So, let me finish with this:

First, definitely no more bad boys. They just grow up into bad men, who are trifling. So, avoid them like the plague. Remember that people, deep down, never change. They may become consummate actors, but they are just acting, they are still the same inside. Once a SOB, always a SOB. Never make someone or something feel small, that's what bullies do, and bullies are nothing but worthless cowards. Go ahead and cry when something is sad, or kind, or happy, or brave. And remember what my mother said: What is in your heart, will, as you age, show up in your face. So, be good and honest and kind. Also, I have learned that sometimes you do have to give up. And that you should never "cast thy pearls before swine" because they will trample over your goodness, then turn around and squash and destroy what is you. And finally, always face what you fear. For, if you do, you are not only brave, you are also free.

JULY 1960